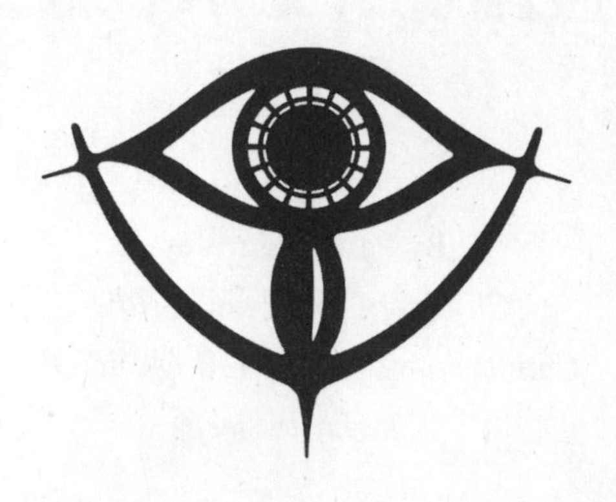

OTHER BOOKS BY TREMBLAY & WALLACE

By Paul Tremblay

City Pier: Above and Below

Compositions for the Young and Old

The Little Sleep

By Sean Wallace

Best New Fantasy

Horror: The Best of the Year, 2006 Edition (with John Gregory Betancourt)

Jabberwocky 1, 2, and 3

Jabberwocky 4 (with Erzebet Yellowboy)

Japanese Dreams

Weird Tales: The 21st Century (with Stephen H. Segal)

Worlds of Fantasy: The Best of Fantasy Magazine (with Cat Rambo)

By Paul Trembly and Sean Wallace

Bandersnatch

Fantasy

Phantom

PHANTOM

Edited by
PAUL TREMBLAY
and SEAN WALLACE

PRIME BOOKS

PHANTOM

Cover and interior design / typesetting by
Linduna [www.linduna.com]

Prime Books
www.prime-books.com

For more information, contact Prime.

ISBN: 1-60701-200-6

To both of our wives, for being understanding and patient.

—Paul and Sean

TABLE OF CONTENTS

LITERARY HORROR:
Dude, you made that up!

The following is a brief (and clearly informal!) e-mail exchange with a colleague—who primarily writes and reads works of fantasy—concerning **PHANTOM** and horror in general:

> **Colleague:** A horror anthology sounds interesting. I'm a person who loves/hates horror. I can't read or watch movies without getting the heebie-jeebies. Yet, I still do it (on rare occasion).
>
> **Me:** I'm a big time scaredy cat. So my tastes tend to be particular; "literary horror" if there's such a thing.
>
> **Colleague:** "Literary Horror" . . . Dude, you made that up! But I think you mean something more psychological than gross out/painful being the result. Or do I have that wrong? I don't like horror for the sake of having lots of death. I like some deeper reason (more than he was crazy).

All right, so horror has its baggage: the seemingly unending stream of exploitative Hollywood slasher and torture movies, the stuff of pubescent revenge and misogynistic fantasies, or the retread plot of some unspeakable horror visits the nice white suburban neighborhood and the 'other' must be defeated; and most recently, the seemingly unending horde of Internet champions, websites with names like StabbyStabStab.com that feature unreadable stories and slime-lined banner-ads to their vanity published books, their authors boasting of being the next Stephen King or being too-brutal-for-your-grandma. As frustrating as it is, no other genre seems to be as defined or recognized by the works that fail as art.

Yeah, there's baggage with both words (literary and horror), and yeah, there's a lot of bad horror but, Dude, I did not make up "literary horror." I swear. It lives! Within the last half-century practitioners of literary horror include Shirley Jackson, William Faulkner (tell me "A Rose for Emily" is not a horror story, go ahead, I dare you!), Flannery O'Connor, Joyce Carol Oates, Stewart O'Nan, Chuck Palahniuk, and Kelly Link just to name a few.

Many a more qualified writer has attempted an in-depth defintion of the genre, but here's an incredibly brief and awkward attempt at defining literary horror (I could be rightly accused of simply describing horror that I like . . . but since you're reading this, you're stuck with it!) by what it achieves: The literary horror story aims to do more than shock, titilate, scare, or affect the reader. While affect is a clear and important (possibly defining) element of horror fiction, there needs to be more. In using the elements of literary fiction—style, theme, setting, character—the literary horror story goes beyond the scare, beyond the revealing of some terrible truth (personal or social or universal) and asks the truly terrifying questions: What's next? What decisions are you going to make? Does it matter the consequences? Do you know the consequences? How are you going to live through this? How does anyone live through this? Stories where the shock or the grand revealings or implications aren't the point, but just a part of the exploration of how people react to the everyday horrors of existence, how they might answer *How does anyone live through this?*

The true horrors of the inimitable Steve Rasnic Tem's "The Cabinet Child" are the decisions Alma and her husband make, independently of each other, while under the duress of an all-too-familiar loneliness.

Steve Eller's "The End of Everything" and Carrie Laben's "Invasive Species" present recognizable but fresh apocalyptic scenarios, making their settings painfully personal via the desperate actions of their flawed and fragile characters.

In the break-neck paced "The Ones Who Got Away," Stephen Graham Jones tells us right up front that something bad is going to happen, and makes us live through the hours of decisions and consequences (both intended and unintended) leading up to the inevitable.

Michael Cisco's wonderfully unreliable narrator in "Mr. Wosslynne" spins a dizzying Aickman-like fever dream that blurs reality and identity. Similar in its unreality, Becca De La Rosa's story pieces the bits of Kate's life together creating ghosts and houses, and nothing is safe.

From paranoid gold prospectors to lonely curators, Satan-worshiping Long Island teens, metaphysics-obsessed television reporters, and to Peter and Olivia and their devastating final choices detailed in the last pages of this anthology, the fourteen stories of **Phantom** present their horrors differently, but they all ask: *How does anyone live through this?*

Paul Tremblay
7/30/09

PHANTOM

THE CABINET CHILD

Steve Rasnic Tem

Around the beginning of the last century, near a small southwest Virginia town which no longer exists, a childless woman named Alma lived with her gentleman farmer husband in a large house on a ridge on the outskirts of this soon-to-be-forgotten town. The woman was not childless because of any medical condition—her husband simply felt that children were "ill-advised" in their circumstances, that there was no space for children in the twenty-or-so rooms of what he called their modest home.

Not being of a demonstrative inclination, his wife kept her disappointment largely to herself, but it could not have been more obvious if she had screamed it from their many-gabled roof. Sometimes, in fact, she muttered it in dialog with whoever should pass, and when no one was looking, she pretended to scream. Over the years despair worked its way into her eyes and drifted down into her cheeks, and the weight of her grief kept her bent and shuffling.

Although her husband Jacob was an insensitive man he was not inobservant. After enduring a number of years of his wife's sad display he apparently decided it gave an inappropriate impression of his household's tenor to the outside world and became determined to do something about it. He did not share his thinking with her directly, of course, but after an equal number of years enduring his maddening obstinacy his wife was well acquainted with his opinions and attitudes. Without so much as a knock he came into her bedroom one afternoon as she sat staring out her window and said, "I have decided you need something to cheer yourself up, my dear. John Hand will be bringing his wagon around soon and you may choose anything on it. Let us call it an early Christmas present, why don't we?"

She looked up at him curiously. After having prayed aloud for some sign of his attention, for so many nights, she could scarcely believe her ears. Was this some trick? As little as it was, still he had never offered her such a prize before. She thought at first that somehow he had hurt his face, then realized what she had taken for a wound was simply a strained and unaccustomed smile. He carried that awkward smile out the door with him, thank God. She did not think she could bear it if such a thing were running around loose in her private quarters.

John Hand was known throughout the region as a fine furniture craftsman who hauled his pieces around in a large gray wagon as roughly made as his furniture was exquisitely constructed. And yet this wagon had not fallen apart in over twenty years of travels up and down wild hollows and over worn mountain ridges with no paved roads. She had not perused his inventory herself, but people both in town and on the outlying farms claimed he carried goods to suit every taste and had a knack for finding the very thing that would please you, that is, if you had any capacity for being pleased at all, which some folk clearly did not.

Alma had twenty rooms full of furniture, the vast majority of it handed down from various branches of Jacob's family. Alma had never known her husband to be very close to his relations, but any time one of them died and there were goods to be divided he was one of the first to call with his respects. And although he was hardly liked by any of those grieving relatives he always seemed able to talk them into letting him leave with some item he did not rightly deserve.

Sometimes at night she would catch him with his new acquisitions, stroking and talking to them as if they had replaced the family he no longer much cared for. She could not understand what had come over her that she would have married such a greedy man.

Although she needed no furniture, without question Alma was sorely in need of being pleased, which was why she was at the front gate with an apron pocket full of Jacob's money the next time John Hand came trundling down the road in that horse-drawn wagon full of his wares.

Even though she waved almost frantically Hand did not appear to acknowledge her, but then stopped abruptly in front of their grand gate. She had seen him in town before but never paid him much attention. When Hand suddenly jumped down and stood peering up at her she was somewhat alarmed by the smallness of the man—he was thin as a pin and painfully bent, the top of his head not even reaching to her shoulders, and she was not a particularly tall woman. The wagon loomed like a great ocean liner behind him, and she could not imagine how this crooked little man had filled it with all this furniture, pieces so jammed together it looked like a puzzle successfully completed.

Then Mr. Hand turned his head rather sideways and presented her with a beatific smile, and completely charmed she felt prepared to go with anything the little man cared to suggest.

"A present from the husband, no?"

"Well, yes, he said I could choose anything."

"But not the present madam most wished for." He said it as if it were undeniable fact, and she did not correct him. Surely he had simply guessed, based on some clues in her appearance?

He gazed at her well past the point of discomfort, then clambered up the side of the wagon, monkey-like and with surprising speed. The next thing she knew he had landed in front of her, holding a small, polished wood cabinet supported by his disproportionately large palm and the cabinet's four unusually long and thin, spiderish legs. "I must confess it has had a previous owner," he said with a mock sad expression. "She was like you, wanting a child so very much. This was to be in the nursery, to hold its dainty little clothes."

Alma was alarmed for a number of reasons, not the least of which that she'd never told the little man that she had wanted a child. Then she quickly realized what a hurtful insult this was on his part—to give someone never to have children a cabinet to hold its clothes? She turned and made for the gate, averting her head so the vicious little man would not see her streaming tears.

"Wait! Please," he said, and a certain softness in his voice stopped her more firmly than a hand on her shoulder ever could. She turned just as he shoved the small cabinet into her open arms. "You will not be—unfulfilled by this gift, I assure you." And with a quick turn he had leapt back onto the seat and the tired-looking horses were pulling him away. She stood awkwardly, unable to speak, the cabinet clutched to her breast like a stricken child.

In her bedroom she carried the beautifully-polished cabinet with the long, delicate legs to a shadowed corner away from the window, the door, and any other furniture. She did not understand this impulse exactly; she just felt the need to isolate the cabinet, to protect it from any other element in her previous life in this house. Because somehow she already knew that her life after the arrival of this delicate assemblage of different shades of wood would be a very different affair.

Once she had the cabinet positioned as seemed appropriate—based on some criteria whose source was completely mysterious to her—she sat on the edge of her bed and watched it until it was time to go downstairs and prepare dinner for her husband. Afterwards she came back and sat in the same position, gazing, singing softly to herself for two, three, four hours at least. Until the sounds in the rest of the house had faded. Until the soft amber glow of the new day appeared in one corner of her window. And until the stirrings inside the cabinet became loud enough for her to hear.

She came unsteadily to her feet and walked across the rug with her heart racing, blood rushing loudly into her ears. She held her breath, and when the small voice flowered on the other side of the shiny cabinet wall, she opened its tiny door.

❖

Twenty years after his wife's death Jacob entered her bedroom for the third and final time. The first time had been the afternoon he had strode in to announce his well-meant but inadequate gift to her. The second time had been to find her lifeless body sprawled on the rug when she had failed to come down for supper. And now this third visit, for reasons he did not fully understand, except that he had been overcome with a terrible sadness and sense of dislocation these past few weeks, and this dusty bed chamber was the one place he knew he needed to be.

He would have come before—he would have come a thousand times before—if he had not been so afraid he could never make himself leave.

He had left the room exactly as it had been on Alma's last day: the covers pulled back neatly, as if she planned an early return to bed, a robe draped across the back of a cream-upholstered settee, a vanity table bare of cosmetics but displaying an antique brush and comb, a half-dozen leather-bound books on a shelf mounted on the wall by her window. In her closet he knew he would find no more than a few changes of clothes. He didn't bother to look because he knew they betrayed nothing of who she had been. She had lived in this room as he imagined nuns must live, their spare possessions a few bare strokes to portray who they had been.

It pained him that it was with her as it had been with everyone else in his life—some scattered sticks of furniture all he had left to remember them by—where they had sat, what they had touched, what they had held and cared for. He had always made sure that when some member of the family died he got something, any small thing, they had handled and loved, to take back here to watch and listen to. And yet none was haunted, not even by a whisper. He knew—he had watched and listened for those departed loved ones most of his adult life.

His family hadn't wanted him to marry her. No good can come, they said, of a union with one so strange. And though he had loved his family he had separated from them, aligning himself with her in this grand house away from the staring eyes of the town. It had not been a conventional marriage—she could not abide being touched and permitted him to see her only at certain times of the day, and even then he might not even be present as far as she was concerned, so intent was she on her conversation with the people and things he could not see.

His family virtually abandoned him over his choice, but as a grown man it was his choice to make. He was never sure if his beloved Alma had such choices. Alma had been driven, apparently, by whatever stray winds entered her brain.

The gift she had chosen in lieu of a child (for how could he give his child such a mother, or give his wife such a tender thing to care for?) still sat in its corner in shadow, appearing to lean his way on its insubstantial legs. He perceived a narrow crack in the front surface of the small cabinet, which drew him closer to inspect the damage, but it was only that the small door was ajar, inviting him to secure it further, or to peek inside.

Jacob led himself into the corner with his lantern held before him, and grasping the miniature knob with two trembling fingers pulled it away from the frame, and seeing that the door had a twin, unclasped the other side and spread both doors like wings that might fly away with this beautiful box. He stepped closer then, moving the light across the cabinet's interior like a blazing eye.

The inside was furnished like some doll's house, and it saddened him to see this late evidence of the state of Alma's thinking. Here and there were actual pieces of doll furniture, perhaps kept from her girlhood or "borrowed" from some neighbor child. Then there were pieces—a settee very like the one in this room, a high-backed Queen Anne chair—carved, apparently, from soap, now discolored and furred by years of clinging dust and lint.

Other furniture had been assembled from spools and emery boards, clothespins, a small jewelry box, then what appeared to be half a broken drinking cup cleverly upholstered with a woman's faded black evening glove.

He was surprised to find in one corner a small portrait of himself, finely painted in delicate strokes, and one of Alma set beside it. And underneath, in tiny, almost unreadable script, two words, which he was sure he could not read correctly, but which might have said "Father," "Mother."

He decided he had been hearing the breathing for some time—he just hadn't been sure of its nature, or its source. The past few years he had suffered from a series of respiratory ailments, and had become accustomed to hearing a soft, secondary wheeze, or leak, with each inhalation and exhalation of breath. That could easily have been the origin of the sounds he was hearing.

But he suspected not. With shaking hand he reached into the far corner of the box, where a variety of handkerchiefs and lacy napkins lay piled. He peeled them off slowly, until finally he reached that faint outline beneath a swatch of dress lace, a short thing curled onto itself, faintly moving with a labored rasp.

He could have stopped then, and thought he should, but his hand was moving again with so little direction, and just nudged that bit of cloth, which dropped down a bare quarter inch.

Nothing there, really, except the tiny eyes. Tissue worn to transparency, flesh vanished into the dusty air, and the child's breathing so slight, a parenthesis, a comma. Jacob stared down solemnly at this kind afterthought, shadow of a shadow, a ghost of a chance. Those eyes so innocent, and yet so old, and desperately tired, an intelligence with no reason to be. Dissolving. The weary breathing stopped.

In the family plot, what little family there might be, there by Alma's grave he erected a small stone: "C. Child" in bold but fine lettering. There he buried the cabinet and all it had contained, because what else had there been to bury? Two years later he joined them there, on the other side.

THE END OF EVERYTHING

Steve Eller

A priest, talking about *World Without End,* that's all I have left from a childhood of Sundays. Sweating in my miniature black suit, clip-on tie dangling from a starched collar. My family's voices, singing and testifying, were just background noise for those three words. Yanking my wayward mind back from daydreams of chasing goldbugs or sharpening knives, fixing me to the pew like cold metal through the heart. Just like the nails in the glistening Christ above the priest. I remember raising my hands, to see if I was dripping blood too.

If that priest was here with me now, I'd carve those words into his face, and see what dripped out of him. Not that it would do any good. Not for me, and certainly not for him.

When was the last time I saw glass that wasn't broken? It's nothing but spiderweb cracks now, or jagged shards like teeth. I wonder if there's one smooth pane left anywhere, to gleam like a sheet of fire in the sun. Or rim the world in frost.

The city street below me is empty. Unless there's some word beyond empty. Everything gleams a greasy grey. There's no sun peeking through the constant clouds, which isn't unusual for Ohio in wintertime. I'm just not sure it's still winter. It might be early morning or midnight. It could be tomorrow or yesterday.

I lean through the window frame, looking straight up. With so much grey I lose my perspective, slipping toward vertigo. It would be so easy to just let go, surrender my balance and tumble out. It's not the first time I've thought about it. But I'm afraid of what might happen. Almost as much as what might not.

Just like the rest of the world, the sky is dead. A fragment of a song pops into my head. Three words again. *Dead Ohio Sky.* I can't remember the rest.

Ninth Street runs straight to the lakefront, where the horizon is all water from my twentieth-story view. Lake Erie is choppy and frothed with white, though there's no wind. If not for the waves, there'd be nothing to distinguish water from sky. I used to stare out this window-hole, wondering when a ship would sail up, full of experts who'd climb on shore. Soldiers and scientists who knew what went wrong, people who could help me, in more ways than one. But they never came. And the world never got fixed.

This building used to be offices, and the walls are lined with roll-front bookcases. They were full of binders, some kind of financial records. I took them all out and threw them down the stairwell, replaced them with food and water. I grab a random can and pull the zip-top. Whatever's inside is orange as clown hair. It could be chili or soup, maybe dog food. The electricity is still on in the building and there's a microwave down the hall in a break-room, but that's too much trouble. It's just food, after all. Fake-colored chunks of slimy meat. Warmth won't make it taste good. I grab a plastic spoon.

When it all started ending, I stocked up on water and canned goods. Everyone else was busy panicking, getting their stupid selves killed. But I can't criticize them too much. They can't be as used to death as me. I've spent my life around it. So while they were screaming and running, I was looting stores and lugging crates up twenty flights, making myself a safe and secret place. I figured I'd be Vincent Price in that old movie. The last person on the planet, with all the monsters out to get me.

After a few tasteless mouthfuls, I shoulder the fire-door open. Can and spoon go down the stairwell. I don't hear them hit bottom. The meal sits in my belly like a stone, and I figure walking might grind it down to pebbles. The elevator in the hallway is open and waiting, since I'm the only one who uses it. I wish I had've known it was still working when I was carrying cases of water up the stairs. I tap the button for *Lobby* and the door shuts behind me. Machinery clanks and sputters inside the paneled walls, until the car jolts to a stop at the bottom. The elevator can't be safe to use, and may kill me one day. But somehow, I doubt it.

"Hey, mister," a soft voice said. "What's your hurry?"

Staying still was hard. The night wind was cold enough to bite through wool and skin. *Cold as God's heart*, I thought. There was a knife in my coat pocket, and I pricked my thumb.

Penance, for thinking such a thing, no matter how true. Moving was the only way to keep warm. But the voice brought me to a stop.

A tangle of highway overhead, ramps and interchanges. Tires rumbled and whined. In the shadows beneath, people huddled around a trashcan fire. All scarves and hats, it was hard to tell them apart. Bits of metal and glass littered the ground, twinkling in firelight. The one who spoke stood away from the others. A thin, hunched figure, rubbing ragged gloves together. There was enough light to see it was a young girl.

"It's cold out tonight," she said. "Take me home."

She had a knit cap pulled down to her eyebrows and the hood of her quilted coat was up. But I saw her face. She might've been born like that. Maybe she was burned, or her family threw her from a moving car like an unwanted pet. The ruined skin made her smile too beautiful, and I thanked Heaven for the strand of shadow she passed through. Her scent was unwashed flesh and the acid breath of an empty stomach, but her eyes were clear and hard like the icicles hanging from the guardrail.

I wondered what could've brought this child to Cleveland in the dead of winter. Her life story had to be a tragedy, like her face. But I didn't wonder why she called out to me, instead of the other dark shapes along the street. Fate is a story all its own.

"How old are you?" I asked.

"What are you, a cop?"

"No. I'd just like to know."

"Old enough to make it worth your while."

It touched my heart that such perfection could exist in the world. In this tiny creature, waiting in frigid darkness, willing to trade herself for warm air.

"So cruel," I whispered.

"Huh?"

"Creation without hope of redemption."

"Hey, look. Do you want to take me home, or not?"

I wrapped her in my arms, and she didn't resist. She raised her face, like offering me a kiss. One of my hands touched her cheek, so she didn't speak anymore. Her spoiled skin was rough as corduroy. My other hand left the knife in my pocket.

"You are home."

I've seen the lobby countless times, but it's still a sight. Like a war zone, where the battle's over but nobody's left to pick up the pieces. There's dry blood across the floor, ink-black. And more is sprayed on the walls. In places it's like a stencil, an outline of the person who bled there, or more burst than bled, maybe. I heard there were stencils like this in Japan after the atomic bomb. People burned so fast they left a human imprint scorched in stone. Bloodstains would take longer to set. There are piles of leaves and trash in every corner, but no bodies. They either got dragged away, or stood up and left on their own.

The revolving door is nothing but a metal frame. I turn it, though I could just as easily step right through. The city is silent. I never realized, before it all ended, how noisy the world used to be. Now there's no cars or buses, no airplanes humming overhead. No human voices chattering nonsense into cell phones. The silence was overwhelming at first, and I'd squeeze my head in my hands to keep it from splitting like a dropped pumpkin.

The lakefront is the only place worth going. Nothing happens there, but at least there's movement. The quiet of the world is broken by my boots smacking the sidewalk. Every storefront I pass has shattered windows, and I catch my reflection in the fragments. My hair is long now, breaking over my shoulders. It must take months, if not a year, for it to grow to this length. I stop for a better look, amazed at how much white is creeping into my beard. The little eye in my head still sees me as the same person, but somewhere along the line I've been getting old.

Two blocks from the lake, I hear them, stirring nearby. Who knows how many. A warning jangles down my spine. It's an instinct as old as time, rational mind giving in to the ways of meat and bone. There's nothing to be afraid of, but the ancient part of my brain, the lizard-jelly, will never be convinced.

Maybe it's because I'm not carrying a knife. That's something I haven't been able to say since kindergarten. Hiding a knife on me was part of getting ready to go out into the world. The sure weight of a switchblade in my pocket. The chill of an eight-inch carver up the sleeve of my overcoat. Before the world ended, I had it all worked out. A knife was part of me. Cold, hard metal was the perfect complement to soft, warm skin.

They don't make any sound. Not with their mouths or throats. But with the city so silent, I hear them coming closer. Feet dragging on asphalt, liquid spattering from their sodden clothes. With no wind, it's hard to smell them until they're near enough to touch. My skin tingles, the muscle underneath bunching to run, to save itself. But all I do is turn around and look.

The girl warmed herself by the radiator while I heated milk on the stove. She peeled off clothes as she lost her chill. First her gloves, then her coat. A flannel shirt, several sizes too big, fell onto the pile at her feet. It was a man's shirt, and I wondered how she bargained to get it.

"Do you like marshmallows with your cocoa?"

"Sure," she replied. "Whatever you got."

Her back was to me and I watched long, straight hair tumble down when she removed her cap. Too black to be anything but from a bottle. And recently dyed. Such a slice of the human heart, that she was capable of vanity while living under a highway.

I poured steaming milk into two mugs and stirred until brown powder dissolved. I couldn't find any marshmallows, but didn't think she'd care. I took the two mugs and carried them into the living room. She was down to a threadbare tank-top and jeans. Toes obvious through worn-out socks.

"Thanks," she said, cradling her mug in hands barely big enough to surround it. "This is a first."

"How so?"

"Usually somebody just hands me their . . . "

"We don't need to talk about that," I said.

She sipped, and I heard her stomach gurgle. It takes a while for a belly to get that empty. I couldn't tell which she liked more, the taste of the chocolate or the heat of the mug. I was barely started with my drink when she slurped the dregs of hers.

"That was good," she said, turning back to the radiator, still holding the mug.

I saw a ring of bruises around both her arms, the pattern like fingers. But there was no damage, like to her face. Her breathing was heavy and I wondered if there was a disease eating away her lungs. I could hear her heart. Or maybe it was just my own.

She was such a symbol of how callous God was. To make life and let it go its own way. Then let it end. But what does God know about dying? He leaves that to his children.

"So do you want to get started?" she asked.

"Like you said to me, what's your hurry?"

She turned around, locking her eyes to mine. Her shoulders were so thin, almost pointed. She seemed fragile, hollow-boned as a bird, like I could crush her in my bare hands. But life is never so easy to take.

"What are you," she asked, smiling gently, "one of those nice guys?"

"Far from it."

"You're not gonna try and help me, or save me?"

"I'll help you. Who knows if it'll save you."

"Not even gonna offer me a sermon?"

"Nope. Just a hot shower."

There's a line of them, maybe a dozen, coming out of an underground parking garage. I can't imagine what they were doing down there. At the head of the column is a young woman. She's coming straight at me, left hand raised, the other cradling her belly. Her eyes are gazing off toward the sky. It's unnerving, like interacting with a disabled person who uses senses in a different way.

She's in good shape. All her limbs attached, her clothes intact. Her skin is a pale grey, so she must've come back recently. The line behind her is a chronology. The further back, the older and more decayed they are. Maybe they move slower, or maybe they have less reason to approach me. On the shadowed ramp, the ones at the back are already turning and heading down again. They must've been through this before. Some of them look familiar. The girl must be new in more ways than one.

When she's an arm's-length away, she's the only one left. The others have all turned away, disappearing into the garage. This near, I see the cuts inside her arms. Long-ways, from wrist to elbow. She knew what she was doing. There's not even any blood on her t-shirt. Her wounds tell me all I need to know. She lived for a while, then ended her own life. She wasn't one of mine.

The girl stops, leans toward me. Her right arm, tight against her body, must be broken. There's nothing spilling out of her belly to hold inside. Maybe the arm was paralyzed while she lived. Her left hand comes close to my cheek and I feel the chill of her fingers. Mouth open, she tilts her head. Her gums are the color of dough. She has no breath, but her smell is old meat between teeth.

I've seen them kill so many times. The sudden burst of violence from their seemingly brittle bodies, fingers and mouths ripping chunks of meat they chew but never swallow. Driven by some strange instinct, or simple desire.

Her eyes could belong to a steamed fish, white and gelid. They roll down from the sky, meeting mine. But it's not sight, just coincidence. She doesn't move away, but her mouth shuts. I hear a sharp click where her jaw closes wrong. There's no blood in her, and her brain must be a puddle in her skull. But she's made her decision, and it's the same one all the others made.

"What am I to you?"

My voice doesn't keep her from turning away. They don't hear or see. No breath, so they don't know scents. I saw one of them without a tongue continue to eat, so they don't taste. But something draws them to people, and makes them walk away from me.

"What are you to me?"

When she's gone, I finish my walk to the waterfront. There are benches facing the lake and I pick one solely by proximity. The waves beat against the pier, moved by a power as mysterious as the dead girl's judgment. Sky and water, grey on grey, seem like one solid mass. I wonder if I stepped onto the waves, if I could walk across like Jesus. But even a messiah needs somewhere to go.

❖

"I was wondering when you'd get here."

Her outline was a blur through the shower curtain, but her intent was clear. Steam billowed over the rod, clouding on the ceiling, smudging my reflection in the bathroom mirror. I figured she was enjoying the hot water. That's why she was gone so long. But she was waiting, certain I'd come in and join her. Like she needed to get this done now, so she could sleep under a ramp instead of in a warm bed.

When I slid the curtain back, she didn't so much as flinch. Her hair was soaked to a point at the small of her back. Her skin was pink as smoked pork. Eyes like gems in a stark desert of a face. Her starved body was flawless. Her only damage was to the thing all the world could see. Maybe that's why she was so eager to show the rest.

"Get your clothes off, already. And hop in. You're letting in a draft."

"I just want to look," I said. *At God's Work.*

"If you like to watch," she whispered, fingers moving over her skin.

My fingers moved, too. Into my pants pocket, around the handle of the knife. And it was over before she could raise a hand. She slumped and I caught her, helped her down into the tub. She curled like a child about to be born. I closed the curtain. The hot water would wash her blood clean, then away.

On my way back, I stop at the mouth of the parking garage. Staring down the dark ramp, listening. There's no sound of them moving, no sign of the dead girl. The rest must've followed her before. Now she's learned her lesson.

I take a few steps down the ramp, curious what could be below. Are they milling in the dark, waiting? Are they curled up, resting on the asphalt like sleepy babies? Do they need to save what remains of their rotten muscle for the next living thing to pass by? They could be sitting in cars for all I know, dreaming.

Relief sweeps through me as I walk back up the ramp, but it's only instinct. A basic need to be safe. My rational mind knows I could stop and sleep in the middle of the street. I wonder if I should look for someplace else to live. Closer to the water. Maybe I will, when the food is gone. That way, I won't have to carry it all back down. There's no reason for me to live in a hideaway, behind locked firedoors. I've never seen them climb stairs. And even if they could, they have no interest in me. Maybe I never needed to leave my ground-floor apartment.

Next time I walk to the lake I'll make a trip along the shoreline, and pick one of the abandoned mansions. There could be a comfy king-size bed to sleep on, instead of a carpeted office floor. There could be champagne and gourmet food. And a bucket and mop, in case the previous owners left a mess.

I spread plastic over the bathroom tile, the kind movers use. It clung to the floor and never curled at the corners. And it stuck to itself when it was time to ball it all up. I always kept a roll handy.

The air was cool, with no more steam. She must've used up all the hot water. My shoulder brushed the shower curtain as I unraveled more plastic, and it felt as cold as her breath, when I held her close under a highway. One more strip of plastic and there was enough to hold her. I trimmed it with my knife. A few red flecks dotted the seam, delicate as snowflakes. I thought I cleaned the blade better. Metal rings shrieked on the rod when I pushed the curtain open. It was freezing inside the shower and I shut off the water. I closed the knife and slid it back into my pocket.

She looked so small in death, like her miserable life made her larger. Bloodless pale, she could've been a porcelain statue. This was the gift I gave her. Something her creator could never imagine. Mercy.

I reached down to lift her out, and her eyes opened. I tumbled onto my back, and my wet fingers couldn't get any traction on the plastic. All I could do was watch as she stood, glaring down at me. There wasn't a hint of blood on her gaping throat. Her eyes kept going down, rolling to pure white. Her arms came up, hands curled like she was still holding her mug. She took a step, but couldn't lift her legs high enough to climb out of the tub. Instead, she toppled over, right toward me. On the way down, I saw her mouth open.

She was cold and wet, pale like some deep-sea thing. Heavier than I imagined, for a tiny girl with no blood in her. All her frigid weight was on me, and there was a wiry strength in her limbs. I couldn't get enough friction on soaked plastic to push her off. There was a clicking close to my ear, maybe fingernails on tile, maybe teeth on teeth. Her arms and legs pumped franticly, until she slid right off me.

I grabbed her hair, used her momentum to turn myself over. She was standing by the time I got to my knees. Pure reflex, I had the knife in my hand before I was on my feet. She wasn't moving, water pattering from her fingertips onto plastic. But I wasn't taking any chances. I jumped up. Two quick slashes, one to each side of her neck.

This had never happened before. Maybe I got careless. Or faithless.

She didn't weaken or fall. I opened her throat earlier in the shower, and the new neck-wounds completed a crooked letter *H*. But there was nothing left in her to seep from the cuts. She was dead, but not at peace. And there was nothing I could do.

She took a step toward me, and I lifted the knife again. I was running out of places to cut her, but it was all I can think to do. Her bare feet squeaked on plastic as she moved, but she bumped past me, out the bathroom door. I followed her, knife still in front of me. Naked, she walked to my front door. Breathless, I opened it for her.

❖

They huddle around me. I'm only a few miles from the city, but I've never seen any of them. And obviously, they've never been near me. There must be twenty, all ages, rags of designer clothes hanging on their limbs. One woman still wears a diamond necklace. There's a man who must've been a sports star. Seven feet tall and broad as a wall, his clothes are still baggy. All the local heroes lived on the lake.

They each take a turn rushing up to me, then turning away. I stand still and wait for them to finish. Then I can get back to searching the mansion. It's got the largest deck I've ever seen, facing the water. I could live here, and pretend to watch the sunrise.

The crowd thins quickly, only a few stragglers coming up to me. Inside the house their smell is thick, clinging to my tongue like bacon-grease. After they're gone, I'll have to open up all the windows and let the place air out. But I'll keep the first floor windows shut, long-term, so newcomers don't tumble in. Actual, unbroken glass.

I make my way upstairs to the master bedroom, listening. There might be one of them up here. If so, I'll push them down the staircase. But it's deserted.

The scent of them, so many, has given me a headache. I search the master bath for aspirin. Inside the medicine cabinet, there's nothing but a bottle of sleeping pills. I turn on the cold water, splash my face and take a sip from my cupped palm. Another sip could wash the entire bottle of pills down my throat. But something tells me the only rest I'll be getting is on the master bed.

With so much chaos in the street, there was no need to hide my knife. Any blood I could spill would be lost in the flood. The girl I killed was obvious in the mob, white skin gleaming in streetlamp-light as she rode a struggling man down to the sidewalk. She wasn't the only killer, just the youngest. There were so many, most dressed in faded gowns or robes. And it made sense that if the dead rose, the first would come from hospitals and hospices. The crowd grew, but fewer clouds of breath rose from living mouths.

Something bumped my shoulder and I spun, knife ready. It was an elderly man in pajamas, a torn plastic tube taped to his nose. His teeth were bright red, the same as the throat of the girl in his hands. Two jabs and a slash from my knife, and his eyes were gone and his neck split open. But he kept chewing. The girl was limp, her breathing like bubbles through a straw. The bloody wad in his mouth fell out, and he went in for another bite.

I'd seen enough horror movies to know damaging the brain would stop the living dead. But my knife wasn't thick enough to go through skull-bone. So I searched the street for another weapon. A window suddenly shattered somewhere over my head, glass raining down. I lifted my arms as a shield, but nothing touched me. Huge shards crashed around me onto the sidewalk, and not a scratch. Along with the glass there was a piece of window-frame, long nails exposed. I grabbed it and hit the man on his head, three times. His skull was a soup-bowl, but he wouldn't stop. Not until the girl was dead, and he dropped her, walked away. A moment later, she got up.

She staggered up to me, palms open like begging. There was no way to kill her. No way to help her. I dropped the dripping wood, ready to accept my fate. At that moment, a pack of young boys, all in some kind of scout uniform, dashed by. They screamed, and the girl went after them. Heart hammering, I took the opportunity to run away.

Sitting on my deck, I watch the lake. The waves seem to form out of the colorless sky, vanishing as they hit the shore. Spreading more nothing on the world.

I found a collection of fancy knives in the kitchen, lined up on a magnetic strip. I would've loved to have them, back before everything ended. Now there's no more warm skin. The cold metal means nothing. Everything means nothing.

There's food in the cupboards, and there must be a store nearby. No need to go back for my supplies. I haven't checked the garage yet, but there could be a gassed-up car in there. Ready to take me out of the city. This might be an isolated thing, living people gathered in other places. But I doubt it. The tightness in my belly tells me that it's over. No matter where I go, I'll find the world the same.

I wonder if I stopped eating, if it would make any difference. The dead don't want to kill me. A hail of glass from the sky misses me. I'll bet the bottle of sleeping pills wouldn't make me yawn. And I can't give final peace to the afflicted.

Maybe the preacher was right. *World Without End*. And God gets the final laugh.

A GHOST, A HOUSE

Becca De La Rosa

A house grew in Katie's bedroom. It grew from her pillow, setting roots down into her mattress, and at first it was a cottage for mice. There are important steps to follow, in order to cultivate houses. Katie followed carefully. So that the house would grow up big and strong, she spun her bed around to face the window in the morning and swung it back at night; she misted the house with water from an expensive French perfume bottle; she read it bedtime stories about mansions, island castles, beautiful villas, windows, doors. Katie slept on the floor so her house would have somewhere to sleep. Weeks went by like this. Finally, in winter, the house began to grow, first slowly, and then as if it would never stop. Its thatched roof blossomed out into slates. Windows yawned up, wide and hungry. The house grew ceilings and rain-gutters. On Christmas Day Katie climbed into bed with her house. Its walls were warm, and it breathed like an animal, like a dog, and moaned sometimes in its dreams, one shutter kicking. Katie curled up beside it. The house opened its doors to her sleeping head.

❖

Months ago Katie had had a gentleman caller. He said his name was Jammy, though it wasn't. He played chess in her bedroom at night, handling the white queen with his thin fingers, breathing on its skin for luck. Katie had not known how to play chess, before he came. Katie hadn't even owned a chess set.

The first time he visited, she had asked him who he was, and he'd smiled like a solemn king, or a priest. His hair was neat as a shroud. He told her, "My name is Jammy."

"I don't believe you," Katie said.

"It doesn't matter."

"I don't believe in you."

Jammy smiled wider, like a cat, like a bear trap, his teeth white as bandages, mummies, dead pharaohs. "It doesn't matter."

"I don't even think you're real," Katie said, lifting her chin haughtily.

Jammy said, "Don't lie to me. Don't try to walk through me. I am not an empty room, I am not a picture frame, and I can see when you lie, I can see inside you. Let me teach you a game," he said.

Katie's bedroom was the kingdom of Jammy. He came only at night, his heels so quiet on the floor that they could have been moonlight, his skin the blue-white of porcelain, a fine china teacup. Sometimes he brought presents. Matryoshka dolls. Candy canes. Red wine in thimble glasses. Once he brought a folk harp on his back, and though she pretended not to listen he played all night for Katie, until she fell asleep on his right foot.

"What are you doing here?" Katie asked that first night. Jammy didn't answer. He didn't even smile.

❖

Sometimes Katie dreamed of houses, when she dreamed. They grew in fields like barley. Bred in house-hothouses, rows and rows all breathing together under the breathing air. They circled the telephone wires with shimmering wings like magpies, always too many of them to count, so she never knew what it meant, if she was destined to dream in sorrow or gold. Katie raised little house-children, called them in from the hills when it was time for bed. Why did Katie love the houses, and speak their language? The houses didn't know, or they didn't want to say. They kept their secrets.

He wore black suits, terribly dashing, and leather gloves. His fingers were thin and white. Jammy was his own shadow. Katie didn't know how he came into her home—did he climb in through the window? Slide down the air vent? Slip under the door like light? But he came every night. She learned to recognise his hand on the door. It sounded like an escape artist's final failed trick.

In some past life, a long time ago, Jammy had been a scholar, or an explorer, or a Persian prince. He told stories that owed a lot to Greek mythology. Sisters married their brothers. Men argued with gods. Snakes rose out of the heart of the earth, fire spitting in their diamond-backed skins. He told stories about a girl named Peach. He had known her, he said, before he died. Was Jammy dead? Katie doubted it, but thought anything was possible. What was Jammy? Katie didn't know.

Jammy was not always good. He did not always bring gifts and strange stories. Sometimes he came in soundlessly and bent over her while she lay in bed, his breath hot and dry on her face, his face black. She woke up to find his hands around her neck. She woke up to find him whispering *sternum, calcaneus, clavicle, triquetrum*. Sometimes he smashed books against her windows and screamed. His voice was like a terrible mistake. When he had screamed himself silent he would climb onto the bed beside Katie. She could never bring herself to touch him, and their silence became holy, the inside of her room a cathedral, smoke and space. Jammy did not remember how to apologise.

"I worry about you," Katie said one day, before she knew it was true.

"Please, don't," Jammy said graciously. He waved one graceful gloved hand. "I can take care of myself."

"Don't lie to me," Katie said.

❖

In all the years before Jammy came, Katie had had terrible dreams. She wrote them down in a notebook by her bed, hoping for an exorcism, but they never left. She dreamed about breathing carbon monoxide inside a garage, about fires that snatched at kitchens, babies scooped from bathtubs like glittering blue fish, and it felt like watching a bird die in her hand; the bird had died, but it was the hand that haunted her, that it had held something so terrible. Once when she was seventeen she pushed a blade against her wrist, but the cottage she lived in cried out. The cottage cried her name.

Katie told all this to Jammy, and he nodded, intent as a doctor diagnosing a rare disease. "That's why I'm here," he said. "To guard you from bad dreams. To teach you to listen without drowning. I am a dreamcatcher. I'm here to help you.

Around them, Katie's home shuddered, uneasy, listening.

❖

A few facts about Peach.

Peach lived inside a circle of jack pine and witches broom. She loved piano music and bad art. "I lived in her cupboard," Jammy said, "above the hot press." He made friends with the towels and the washcloths. At night, when the cold came, he slept curled up on the bottom shelf, his cheek pressed against the wood to soak up heat. He spoke the language of furnaces. When he crawled out of the cupboard on all fours every morning, it was like being born clean. Peach fed him almonds and milk and honey. She was not particularly beautiful, but she had a holy look, some kind of Mary. Peach dressed Jammy in silk and soft leather and sent him out in the world to do good among strangers.

Katie wanted to know if it was Peach who taught Jammy to

play chess. She wanted to know how Peach lived, if she walked right out of a sacred painting with that halo still hanging off her. Did she find Jammy underneath a horse chestnut tree? Did she grow him from a seed in her cupboard, tucked up warm? Katie wanted to know where Jammy came from and where he went when he went away. Maybe, she thought, he spent his days with Peach still, eating lint and warmth and honey. Katie wanted to ask, were you in love with Peach or were you afraid of her? Where is she now? "We lived side-by-side like organs," Jammy said, thoughtfully, and Katie thought: not the heart but the dead organs of the body, eyeless, nosing their way through the skeleton blind, fish of the veins.

Sometimes the house dreamed. It dreamed about the underground, which had been like a house to it, and about Katie, while it slept on her head like a snug square cap. It dreamed of growing fat as a mansion. It snored sometimes, in its sleep.

Churches haunted the house's dreams. Stained glass. Buttresses. Steeples. In churchyards the dead slept close to the foundations, standing guard. The flagstones had been blessed again and again.

If the house had one wish, it would become a church. It would grow holy around Katie's head. The house dreamed of sprouting a steeple, blooming colours, and it would be beautiful, the cut chunk of a prism when the light shone through it.

Jammy walked across Katie's room with blood on his sleeves like unfortunate cufflinks. They lay on the bed together. Katie could not hear Jammy breathe, could not move close enough to feel the heat from his body. "Why is it so hard for you?" she asked. "How did you know my name, where to find me, how to get into my house? Why are you here?"

Jammy laughed. His voice had gone hoarse. "I'm here because you need me."

"I don't need you."

"What happened when you were seventeen, Katie?"

"Nothing happened," she said.

He took off his black dinner jacket and laid it neatly on the bedside table. He popped all the black buttons on his shirt. When he lay on the bed shirtless, Katie carefully walked her fingers up his ribcage, counting the spaces in between his ribs. She fit her thumbs underneath his collarbones. Jammy had grown thinner in the last few months. His bruises looked like thumbprints, Katie's, a stamp saying *mine*. He turned his head away from her. "Peach had a dollhouse," he said. "She kept it in her kitchen. Someone had made it for a child to play with, but spiders slept in all the bedrooms. It was a home that lived inside her home. The way she was a home, and I lived inside her."

"I'm sick of hearing about Peach," Katie said, although she wasn't. She wanted to know everything. She wanted to ask if he wished she was Peach. If he loved Peach more than he loved her, if he loved her. If he was a dollhouse and Peach was a house, what did that make Katie? "You want to leave," she said instead. Katie was proud of her voice, so calm and matter-of-fact, like a typewriter's voice, click-click-click.

"That's not it."

"No?"

"Never," he said.

She rolled off the bed, stood above him, her arms crossed over her chest, suddenly angry. "I don't want you to stay, anyway."

Jammy laughed. "You want me to stay forever."

"I do not," she said.

He smiled at her, teeth biting into his lip. "I don't believe you."

Katie shoved him off the bed. "Don't tell me what you believe," she said. "You don't know what you believe, you don't know anything. You don't know me. Get out of my house! I don't care what you are, I don't care. It's not even me you want, is it? Get your suit and get your chess set and get out of my house."

Jammy swung to his feet, furious and unbreathing. "Never."

"How dare you," she said, "how dare you act like you can help, like you know everything there is to know. You aren't a ghost. You aren't a dollhouse. You aren't anything. You are nothing except ridiculous. I never asked you to come walking through my bedroom in the middle of the night. I never did. Why won't you just leave me alone?"

Jammy stood very still. His face had gone white, the colour of plaster. "Whatever you say," he said, and left.

A few facts about houses.

They are a race of women. They give birth to the men who build their children; but they also give birth to cocktail parties and domestic violence, and arguments, and Christmases, conceptions, treaties, one-night-stands, magic spells, birthday cakes, ruined dinners, ruined marriages, broken hearts, suicides. Death lives in houses long after the dead are buried. Houses dream of benediction.

When she was seventeen Katie slept with a stranger and became a house for a small death. She took to her bed for a week, wrapped up in her duvet like a fragile bowl shipped across the ocean. She wished for stained-glass windows, those sacred eyes, a holy glimpse into her own body. And then she wished to smash those windows in, and she held a blade to her wrist, until the cottage she lived in screamed her name in a panic, the door slamming again and again. When will you let me go? Katie asked, desperate, sick with the thought of that hand clasped tight around her. The house said: Never. Never. Never. Never. Never.

For the days after Jammy disappeared, Katie dreamed about him all night, awake or asleep. She dreamed he came at her with knives, his mouth a black pool, and she offered her wrists to him like fresh bread. A ghost or a dollhouse, a nightmare, a chess instructor. Maybe, Katie thought, she could invoke him;

so she built a spell on her bedroom floor, and burnt sage in a clay pot beside Jammy's handkerchief and his white chess queen, chanting *Jammy, Jammy, Jammy, Jammy*, until the word sounded French. Katie wrote his name over her thighs with permanent marker. Her whole home swelled to make room for him, though he didn't come. Katie wrote questions in a black notebook. If Jammy used to live inside Peach, what lived inside Jammy? If he was a ghost, how did he die? Where were the scars? She wanted to take a candle to her legs, write *Jammy* in wax or in scorch marks, so that if he lived inside her he could see the light, and follow it out.

Jammy was the ghost of an old churchyard, long dead. Jammy grew inside a sweet bell pepper and came out spitting seeds. He undressed Katie on the floor and lived inside her. He did not; he never touched Katie. Jammy had an old debt to pay. Jammy was dead, but he would come again. He would never come again.

In the middle of the night he knelt by Katie's bed and whispered to her *wake up, I need you to wake up.* She hugged her knees. "Where have you been?" she asked, without looking at him, as if she hadn't spent the days trying to call him out from his hiding place.

"Nowhere."

She said, "I guess I'm sorry."

"Kind of you to say."

Jammy's beautiful dress suit did not quite fit now, hanging off his bones, and it had grown tattered and dusty. The new bruises on his cheeks looked like cigarette burns. Katie kissed his mouth. She kissed his collarbone. "You want to stay," she told him, as though that might make it true, and it did, and he did. "I can't," he said. "I have work to do."

He left. Katie thought about him standing guard in someone else's bedroom, over someone else's sleep. She thought about someone else playing chess with him and losing. She had stolen his dinner jacket, and locked it in a drawer in her wardrobe. In a year, in ten years, when the voices she heard stopped being kind, when they began to blame her, tear at her, the blade would finally go down. And would she see Jammy then? Would he come to meet her with his harp on his back, like a visitor at a train station?

Before he left Jammy gave her a present. It was a bulb shaped like a hammer, dull green and clumped with dirt. Katie planted it under her pillow. It grew in winter; houses love winter. It guarded Katie's dreams while her dreams slept inside it. All through the night, Katie heard the sound of one door slamming, again and again.

THE ONES WHO GOT AWAY

Stephen Graham Jones

Later we would learn that the guy kept a machete close to his front door. That he kept it there specifically for people like us. That he'd been waiting.

I was fifteen.

It was supposed to be a simple thing we were doing.

In a way, I guess it was. Just not the way Mark had told us it would be.

If you're wondering, this is the story of why I'm not a criminal. And also why I pick my pizza up instead of having it delivered.

❖

It starts with us getting tighter and tighter with Mark, letting him spot us a bag here, a case there, a ride in-between, until we owe him enough that it's easier to just do something for him than try to scrounge up the cash.

What you need to know about Mark is what you probably know already: he's twenty-five, maybe, and smart enough not to be in jail yet but stupid enough to be selling out the front door of his apartment.

Like we were geniuses ourselves, though, yeah.

❖

As these things go, what started out as a custody dispute somehow turned complicated, and whoever Mark was in the hole with came to him for a serious favor, the kind he couldn't really say no to. The less he knew, the better.

What he did know, anyway, or at least what he told us, was that somebody needed to have the fear of God placed in them.

This was what he'd been told.

In his smoky living room, I'd looked to Tim and he was already pulling his eyes away, focusing on, I don't know. Something besides me.

The fear of God.

I was stupid enough to ask just what, specifically, that might be.

You see it in all the movies, the next few bits of the story. Or, if you've been there, I guess then you see it pretty much everywhere, even the kid shows.

It's the Story of Man.

Casting it in those terms makes it feel bigger, makes your part in it all feel smaller. Maybe even inevitable, like fate, like an afterschool special where I pick up a cigarette in slow motion when I'm twelve, then the camera backs off me and it's three years later, that cigarette hardly burned, and across from me my best friend since third grade is laughing the way he does when he's not all the way stoned yet, and making up things that would put the real and true fear of God in a person.

Watching a movie like that, I'd lean forward, shake my head no. Tell myself to run.

Across town, of course—this isn't the movie, but me looking back, to what had to have been happening—a little kid named Nicholas is sitting in another living room. His parents'. And they're there, of course, one of them a step-, it doesn't matter which. Not to us.

The things he doesn't know, too. It's like a joke itself.

But maybe it's better that way. Give him a day or two more of just sitting there, thinking the world's a good place to be. That his dad's still the same guy he's supposed to be, the same guy he's always been pretending to be.

If he were telling this, though, here's what he'd say: this is the story of why I threw that brick through that window, over and over, until I went to jail.

What he still wouldn't know would be what really happened that night.

Which isn't to say I do.

By ten, when I knew it was time to be slouching out of Mark's, what we finally hit on as the real and true proper fear of God was to think you're going to die, to be sure this is the end, and then live.

We thought we were helping Mark with his dilemma, of course.

Sitting across from us, he crushed out cigarette after cigarette, squinched his face up as if trying to stay awake. Every few minutes he'd lean his head back and rub the bridge of his nose.

The trick of course was that there couldn't be any bruises or cuts.

Of all the things we'd thought of, the knives and guns and nails and fire and acid and, for some reason, a whole series of things involving the tongue and pieces of wire, the only thing that left a mark on just the mind, not the body, was tape. Duct tape. A dollar and change at the convenience store.

This is how you plan a kidnapping.

Mark's suggestion that it should be us instead of him in the van came down to his knowledge of the law: we were minors. Even if we got caught, it'd get kicked when we turned eighteen.

To prove this, he told us his own story: at sixteen, he'd

killed his stepdad with a hammer because of all kinds of shit involving a sister, and then just had to spend two years in lock-up.

Our objection—mine—was that this was all different: we weren't going to kill anybody.

So, yeah, I was the first one of us that said it: *we*.

If Tim heard it, he didn't look over.

The second part of Mark's argument was What could we really be charged with anyway? Rolling some suit into a van for a joyride?

The third part had to do with a tally he had in his head of bags, cases, rides.

Not counting tonight, of course, he added. Because we were his friends.

The rest of it, the next eighteen hours, are boring. Looking back, I know my heart should have been hammering the whole time, that I shouldn't have been able to talk to my parents in the kitchen.

The truth of it is that there were long stretches in there where I didn't even think about what we were doing that night.

It was just going to be a thing, a favor, nothing. Then we'd have a clean tab with Mark, and Mark would have a clean tab with whoever he owed, and maybe it even went farther up than that.

Nicholas, of course—I call him Nicky now, I guess—he was probably doing all the kid things he was supposed to be doing for those eighteen hours: cartoons, cereal, remote control cars. Baseball in the yard with the old man.

At five after six, Tim called me.

Mark had just called him, from a payphone.

We had a pizza to deliver.

❖

On the pockmarked coffee table in Mark's apartment, all we were going to need: two rolls of duct tape, two pairs of gloves, and an old pizza bag from a place that had shut down when Tim and me'd been in junior high.

The gloves were because tape was great for prints, Mark told us.

What that said to us was that he wasn't setting us up. That he really would be doing this himself, if he didn't want to help us out.

Like I said, we were fifteen.

Tim still is.

The van was a salmon that had floated back downstream. It was primer black, no chrome, so obviously stolen that my first impulse was to cruise the bowling alley, nod to Sherry and the rest of the girls, then just keep driving.

If the van were on a car lot in some stupid comedy, where there's car lots that cater to bad guys, the salesmen would look back to the van a few times for the jittery, ski-masked kidnappers, and keep shaking his head, telling them they didn't want that one, no. That one was only for *serious* kidnappers. Cargo space like that? Current tags? Thin hotel mattresses inside, to muffle sound?

No, no, the one they wanted, it was this hot little number he'd just gotten in yesterday.

Then, when the kidnappers fell in with him, to see this hot little number, one would stay behind, his eyes behind the ski mask still locked on the van.

The reason he's wearing a ski mask, of course, is that he's me.

What I was thinking was that this could work, that we could really do this.

Instead of giving us a map or note or anything, Mark followed us out to the curb, his head ducked into his shoulders the way it did anytime he was outside, like he knew God was watching or something. He told Tim the address, then told Tim to say it back.

2243 Hickory.

It was up on the hill, a rich place.

Sure? Mark asked as we were climbing into the van.

I smiled a criminal smile (this is where just one side of your mouth goes up), didn't answer him.

2243 Hickory. A lawyer's house, probably.

We were supposed to take whoever answered the door. Nothing about it that wasn't going to be easy.

To make it more real, we stopped for a pizza to put in the pizza bag. It took all our money, but this was serious business. Another way to look at it was we were paying twelve dollars for all the weed and beer and gas Mark had burned on our undeserving selves.

In which case it was a bargain.

The smell filled the van.

On the inside of his forearm, like an amateur, Tim had written the address. Instead of 'Hickory,' though, he'd just put 'H.' All he'd have to do would be lick it a couple of times and it'd be gone.

Like *2243H* meant anything anyway.

Then, I mean.

Now I drive past that house at least once a month.

Because records are part of my job now, I know who was living at that house when I was fifteen.

A family. Their name's not important. It's the same as any name.

It was Dickerson, though.

There, I said it.

The Dickersons.

The dad wasn't a lawyer, but a family court judge.

For a long time that didn't make any sense to me, but then, when he finally died, I saw his obituary. Because he'd been a judge, his picture was in there. Maybe it was from that same week, even.

In it, he's just a guy in a big thick robe.

And he's black.

Unlike Nicky, whose blond hair I could see from behind the wheel of the van. He was leaning over, all his weight on one leg, like he could see me too.

And maybe he could.

We finally decided it should be Tim who went to the door. Because he already had a windbreaker on, like pizza guys maybe wore. And because he had an assistant manager haircut. And because I said that I would do all the taping and sit on the guy in the back while we drove around.

How I was going to get the tape started with my gloved fingers, who knew.

How I was going to stop crying down my throat was just as much a mystery.

In the van, Tim walking up the curved sidewalk to the front door, I was making deals with anybody who would listen.

They weren't listening, though.

Or, they didn't hear that I was including Tim in the deals as well.

Or that I meant to, anyway.

As for the actual house we went to, it was 2234 Hickory, not 2243 like it should have been. Just a couple of numbers flipped. Tim would probably just say that he put them in order in his head. If he could still say.

As to what happened with whatever custody case we supposed to be helping with, I never knew, and don't have any idea how to find out.

When I finally made it to Mark's the next week, somebody else answered the door. He had all different furniture behind him, like the girl at the portrait studio had rolled down a different background.

What I did was nod, wave an apology, then spin on my heel—very cool, very criminal—walk away.

What I would be wearing when I did that was a suit, for Tim. Or, for his family, really, who had no idea.

Anything I could have said to them, it wouldn't have helped.

❖

This is the part of the story where I tell about meeting Tim in the third grade, I know. And all our forts and adventures and girlfriends, and how we were family when our families weren't.

But that's not part of this.

I owe him that much.

We should have cruised the bowling alley on the way up the hill that night, though. We should have coasted past the glass doors in slow-motion, our teeth set, our hands out the open window, palms to the outsides of the van doors as if holding them shut.

The girls we never married would still be talking about us. We'd be the standard they measure their husbands against now. The ones who got away.

But now I'm just not wanting to tell the rest.

It happens anyway though, I guess.

Nicky answers the door in his sock feet, and Tim holds the pizza up in perfect imitation of a thousand deliveries, says some made-up amount of dollars.

Then, when Nicky leans over to see the pizza sign on the van (I think), Tim does it, just as Mark played it out for us fifty times: lobs the pizza into the house like a frisbee, so everybody'll be looking at it, instead of him and who he's dragging through the front door.

On top of the pizza, stuck there with a toothpick, is the envelope Mark said we had to leave.

Putting it in the box was our idea.

It was licked shut, but we knew what it said: *if you want whoever we've got back, then do this, that, or whatever.*

As the pizza floated through the door, I saw me in the back of the van with Nicky, playing games until midnight. Making friends. Tim driving and driving.

We were doing him a favor, really. Giving him a story for school.

But then the pizza hit, probably a couple of feet at least.

Mark was twelve miles away, maybe more.

I was only just then realizing that.

❖

The way some things happen is like dominoes falling. Which I know I should be able to say something better, but that's really all it was. Nothing fancy.

Domino one: the pizza lands.

Domino two: Nicky, who'd turned to track the pizza, turns back to Tim, like to see if this is a joke, only stops with his head halfway around, like he's seeing somebody else now.

Domino three: Tim leans forward, to hug Nicky close to him, start running back to the van.

Domino four: what I used to think was the contoured leg of a kitchen table, but now know to be one of those fancy wooden pepper grinders (my wife brought one home from the crafts superstore; I threw up, left the room), it comes fast and level around the frame of the door, connects with Tim's face, his head popping back from it.

Domino five, the last domino: Tim, maybe—hopefully—unconscious, being dragged into the house by Nicky's father, who looks long at the van before closing the door.

❖

The reason I can tell myself that Tim was unconscious is the simple fact that Nicky's father—whose name I didn't have to look up, because it was in all the papers for months and months, and is even in books now— didn't come out for me too. Which is a question he would had to have asked: whether Tim was alone.

So what I do now is just pretend he was knocked out. That he didn't have to feel what happened to him over the next forty-five minutes, like Nicky did. Or saw, anyway. Maybe was even forced to see.

In the papers, it was why Nicky's mom left Nicky's dad: because what he did to the drugged-up kid who broke into their home, he did while Nicky watched.

It involved a kitchen chair, some tape, a hammer. Pliers for the teeth, which he pushed into Tim's earholes and nostrils and tear ducts.

How long I was in the truck was forty-eight minutes.

It's better if Tim was knocked out the whole time.

What people say now—it's still the worst thing to have ever happened—what they say now is that they understand Nicky's dad. That they would have done the same thing. That, once a person crosses the threshold into your house, where you *family* is, that he's giving up every right to life he ever had.

This is what you do if you're a traitor and in the same break room with people saying that: nod.

This is what you do if you hate yourself and can't sleep and have your hands balled into fists under the sheets all night every night: agree with them for real. That, if anybody tries to come in your door one night, then all bets are off.

And then you're a traitor.

Nevermind that, a few months before Nicky's juvenile delinquency bloomed into a five-year stretch with no parole, you went to his apartment, to buy a bag. He was Mark all over, right down to how he narrowed his eyes as he pulled on his cigarette, right down to how he ducked his head into his shoulders like his neck was still remembering long hair. And you didn't use anymore then, hadn't since the night before your wedding, would even stop at the grocery store on the way home, to flush the bag over and over, until the assistant manager knocked on the door, asked if there was a problem.

Yes, there was.

It was a funny question, really.

The problem was that one time while your friend's head was floating across a lawn, a machete glinting real casual in the doorway behind it, a thing happened that you didn't understand for years: the life meant for Nicky, you got. And he got yours.

That's not the funny part, though.

The funny part, the reason the assistant manager finally has to get the police involved in removing you from the bathroom, is that you can still smell the pizza from that night. And that sometimes, driving home to your family after a normal day, you think it was all worth it. That things happen for a reason.

It's not the kind of thing Nicky would understand, though.

Nevermind Tim.

AFTER IMAGES

Karen Heuler

A survey I conducted on Water Street concludes that 58% of Americans think it is probably 58 degrees out, while 22% think it is probably 54, and the remainder aren't sure.

For the first time in weather history this month, the percentage of people thinking it is 58 degrees is exactly 58. This happens, we are told, on average of once every six months. You won't see that happening again until probably late fall or early winter, although polls also show that a majority of people think there won't be any winter next year at all.

That was the gist of my segment on last night's news. Today I got called into the office. "We're getting complaints," the news manager said. He's a fat man and one ear is lower than the other, giving him a quizzical look. "People say your segments are insulting."

"How many people said that? Maybe they're just the kind of people who complain. You have to ask the people who *don't* complain what they think."

"No, I don't," the manager said. "I don't have to do anything."

“Poor choice of words,” I conceded. “I merely meant: balance. We strive for balance.”

“No, we don’t,” the manager said.

“What do you want, sir?” I asked.

“Relevance. Nobody wants a poll on what the temperature might be. They want to know what the temperature *is*, and move on to sports.”

I bowed my head.

And by the way, how accurate are the polls? We asked forty people and twenty said not accurate and twenty said accurate. Which means, according to our off-screen analyst, that any survey, tally, census, or sampling of the public would itself be only half-accurate, since the public is divided in the concept of accuracy itself and is therefore unreliable.

But is this really so? We asked a former employee of Burton & Pudge Poll Company, which compiles statistics on the surveys themselves, how surveys are measured. This employee, who prefers to remain anonymous, says that polls in general get three different results if the interviewee is asked the same question in three different ways. In response, Burton & Pudge representatives stated that this points out the refinements of the polling process, which recognizes that only 30% of respondents hear all the words in a sentence, a figure that has been verified by having test subjects write down all the words in a sentence in reverse order so as to eliminate rote repetition. 10% do not write down the word “not” in a sentence that contains it.

On the other hand, 13% put it in when it wasn't there to begin with.

This is how the polling industry comes up with the plus-or-minus 3% variance, since misunderstandings on either side of the scale are 3% away from canceling themselves out.

I was invited to the office again. The manager said, "That was not what we had in mind. Polls should be fun. If they can't be fun, what's the point of it?"

I considered that, and thought that was a very good observation.

According to research by Wallup and Pye Interview Associates, facial expression is more accurate than verbal expression, at least when the face itself is aware it is lying. Most times it is not lying and then all we want to know is: does a flat face like what we're saying or not? That's simple enough.

Sticking one's tongue out is a no; smiling is a yes, unless the eyes are squinting, in which case it's no again. A shake of the head, no; a nod, yes. But beyond that—what is the nose saying? (Flaring, sniffing, snorting?) We have also calibrated the ears, since some people, sociopaths especially, confine their telling expressions to the earlobe. They may pass all the tests checking the muscles of the lips, the eyebrows, the eyelids, the nostril, but the ear tightens and the lobe clenches. That is a lie.

"The ear?" the co-anchor said, suspiciously.

We can also track your voice, you know; we can tell the truth of what you're saying.

"The ear?" he repeated. "I don't believe the ear even has muscles."

"I don't care about that, really. Maybe it's the cartilage that quivers."

Ha.

He waved me off, also a telling gesture, but a little blunt. It takes no special education to understand that.

I turned to address him, sharing my air time. "Did you know the way you dress also reveals a lot? And I don't mean, do you have style, do you have money. I mean, this is a person who has no imagination, this is a person who fantasizes. Okay, you say, that's easy. But I must add, when you lie, your clothes don't fit as well. Unless you stay absolutely still, and that's a dead giveaway. A person who doesn't shift around during interrogation is a person hiding something."

"Interrogation?"

"Well yes, what did you think I was talking about?"

His eyes narrowed. He slowly put his hand in his pocket. As if he had something, yes. He thought he had an instrument that could deflect me. His nostrils flared. His ear twitched.

I was getting into the hang of being called into the office. I hung my head immediately and said, "Boss, what should I do?"

"You have to know what the public wants," he said. "You

have to have the knack for it. What is it that gets our goat? Scandal, crime, the all-chocolate diet. Death and taxes, they get everyone interested. Do something on taxes."

I'm not interested in taxes.

The final test of any poll of course is what the dead say about dying. That's the poll we want and never get. The dead, as far as polls are concerned, have nothing to say about death once the body freezes up, but right after death, especially that moment we like to call "instantaneous death," we find it is still possible to get a few questions in.

Shortly after a local criminal was guillotined, his head in a basket, a sharply observant reporter noticed that the eyes of the head were slowly closing. He rushed to the head with a microphone.

"Excuse me, sir, how do you feel?" the reporter asked.

The eyes flickered open and stared at the reporter. There was a slight movement of the tongue.

The reporter was excited. "If you feel pain, sir, blink your eyes! Blink on a scale of one to ten to tell us how much pain." He stuck his microphone at the head's lips. Very slowly the eyes looked at the reporter then closed halfway again and stayed there.

The cameraman was standing by the dead criminal's wife, conducting his own interview. "How do you feel now that your husband has been executed, ma'am?" he asked.

But what if the head was lying? He was a criminal, after all.

What if it was nothing more than a bunch of nerve endings firing off without meaning anything? Go back to the science of physiognomy (about which 40% of the population says there is no such science but 60% of the population knows someone or other who can "tell" when someone else is lying) and use its principles to decide whether the decapitated head was telling the truth when it fluttered its eyes.

Physiognomy says a glance to the right means an imaginative thought process. A glance to the left means a recall of memory.

The head glanced to the right. Now, if this were a poker game that would be considered a "tell" if the person did it autonomically in certain situations. Was this a "tell" from the dead head?

In other words, do the dead realize that their opinions still matter?

❖

"Boss?" I asked politely. "Was that what you had in mind?"

"From now on," he said roughly. "No live segments. We're going to review your tapes and decide if they air."

"You didn't like it?" I was shocked.

"There are no guillotine executions in New Jersey," he said. "There never have been guillotine executions in New Jersey."

"Doesn't matter," I said. "The people still need to know."

❖

According to a clairvoyant I consulted, the afterlife is just like this life, only without bodies. The poor are still poor, though this time they are also poor in spirit.

"How does that work?" I asked. "I mean, how can you be poor if there's no money?"

"Oh, there's money," she said. "It just doesn't weigh anything. Besides, *we* put the value on things. It's not like gold has any particular absolute value. We just like it. That's in this world," she said. "There are ten thousand worlds, but not really that much variety. Some are physical, some are spiritual. And they all have rich and poor people."

"What's the point?"

"No point. It simply is. Of course, you'll like it better if you're rich in all the worlds."

"So we *can* bring it with us?" I asked. "How do we prepare to be rich in the next life? Is there some kind of investment opportunity?"

I didn't believe her, of course; I could feel it creeping out of my voice. She was offended.

"You'll learn that your attitude always goes with you," she said stiffly.

I rapped on my table just for the effect. "I think I hear some advice," I said. "Do you know who it's from? I want to do a background check."

And she shut up. That was the end of the segment.

I wouldn't be surprised if there are scams beyond the grave. Some people will believe anything; other people will take advantage of anything.

So, beliefs. What are people willing to believe in? Some

believe they have come from another planet; some believe they are going to one. Some believe they will gain their enemies' strengths by eating their enemies' heart. Others try to claim the soul by, say, sprinkling water on the head or cutting off a bit of skin.

Almost everyone believes in some kind of conspiracy. Like my boss, I think he's working against me.

"You can make fun of the clairvoyants—hell, everyone makes fun of those. But what was that crack about stealing the soul? That was anti-religious. That kills ratings."

"Anti-religious?" I asked, aghast. "I just wanted to point out similarities, you know, parallels."

"Cannibalism and baptism?"

"I'm interested in the metaphysics."

"No."

"No?"

"We're not showing it."

We sat together in a companionable way. "Well, what *can* I cover that has to do with metaphysics?"

"I don't even know what metaphysics is in this day and age," the boss muttered. "But you seem to like death. So I'm putting you in the morgue. Anytime someone dies, you write up the memorial and you find the clips."

"Let me think about it."

"That's really all there is," he said. "And you may have to do some typing besides."

I thought about it. I would still be on-camera, I could talk about the deaths of people who were either admirable or famous; I could wear dark colors, which I like very much. I could roam through photo morgues on company time. I could quote from poems about death. I could insist these dead people held interesting beliefs. Hell, everyone believes in something interesting sometime in their lives.

We need work, meaningful work, if we are to remake all ten thousand worlds. This is what I told the boss. "I'm yours," I said. "But give me a little latitude here. Let me ask how people feel about the death, whether it was the right thing or not."

"The right thing?" his mouth dropped open.

"Sometimes death is wrong," I said sternly.

He stared at me and sighed. "You can give me anything you want, as long as you cover their lifetimes. Do it that way: give me their lives, then give me their deaths."

I was very pleased. "I'll tell you what I think about your death right now," I said.

"No," he said. "I'd like to wait for that."

People once believed that the image of the murderer was etched on the retina of the victim's eyes, like a photographic plate. Like a little camera snapping its own evidence. It must have come from all that "eyes are the mirror of the soul" business. The mirror caught the last reflection and saved it.

No, wait. The eyes are the windows to the soul, I think. So what if it works the other way—the eyes record what the soul sees, it doesn't record what the body sees? No one ever found the murderer's image in the victim's eyes, but did they find something else? Did they see bits and pieces of things that made no sense? A line here, a curve there, none of which added up to anything individually? We are always leaving hieroglyphics, aren't we? Faery stiles, crop circles, Aztec ridges, Nazca lines. Little nicks on cave walls, rocks piled in patterns, dots and dashes. So why not messages for those left behind? It's hard to break that human compulsion to say one more thing.

What if there *are* imprints on the eyes of the dead after all, and they form a message when you put them all together? It's very exciting, when you see a puzzle for the first time; when you sense its solution. Human instinct; human intelligence; the human need to organize information and pass it on. What are polls for but to find the patterns we're secretly storing? What are books and films and TV shows and reports from all over the world except to find the pattern? Who says we would stop the trail, the interpretation, the insight, the comment, when all is said and done? Those who talk never stop talking. Those who reason never stop reasoning.

So I took the job. The boss said Morgues and I went to the morgues—not the library of clippings that he meant but the actual morgues. I spoke to the attendants, who told me that they kept music on to counter their fear of hearing whispers. They don't like the silence because it seems to be waiting. But then they laughed and they winked at each other.

I interviewed them myself and I taped them and I took their pictures. They want to believe they might be famous someday, though we never discussed for what.

"Boss, this is interesting," I said. "They dress the dead and take their pictures. They pose them. The families request it. The families of the long-lost ask to see them in a natural pose."

"Disgusting," he said. "Wait. Maybe an expose?"

But I won't expose them. The attendants let me in after hours. They don't say a word as I open the eyes of the dead and take their picture. I zoom in on the iris, on the retina, I snap them looking back at me on high-speed, on digital. I run home and I blow the photos up, looking for the shapes in the back of their eyes, the shapes that reflect something. Already I have pieced together, from selections of their eyes, the angle of a room, a white room with a doorway and a hall. The doorway has crystal doors, opened and not quite flat to the side. The hallway—I only see a little bit of the hallway and there is a shadow of a hand in it, just beyond the opened door. I can't see who is throwing that shadow. But I will find it out.

My walls are lined with rows and rows of these photos, the blown-up retinas of the dead. They all seem to be looking in the same direction. And in every one of them, there is a clue.

THE LADDER OF ST. AUGUSTINE

Seth Lindberg

"I don't think you get what 'ghost town' means," I told Miguel.

Our car rolled on cracked pavement along a road in a town just south of the Bay Area called San Agosto. The sign hanging over the Rotarian symbols called it THE TOWN OF FREEDOM AND PROSPERITY, something I imagined more of a bald-faced dare than anything else. There were still cars on the roads and in the driveways, the lights still worked, and no one had tore down any of the signs.

"I think your uncle meant the town was haunted," Miguel said, taking a drag off of one of those foul black cigarettes he smoked. "I really do."

He looked worn down from the drive, sunglasses hiding his eyes, his shirt stained from the rather eager way he had devoured the hamburger-and-pineapple-thing sandwich we'd gotten just outside of town, at this fast-food Filipino restaurant. The place did things with spaghetti that countries made treaties just to stop. Miguel goaded me to eat some meat-and-rice thing called a 'Palabok Bandero,' shouting down my Gringo nature with a vicious grin on his face. I was glad to be gone from there and back on the road, but these mazes of twenty-five mile-per-hour streets were getting on my already frayed nerves.

"No," I said, rubbing my temples. I needed more painkillers. I should have taken some at the fast food place, but Miguel was eyeing me, and I didn't want to share. "It's a ghost town meaning the town's deserted."

"But it ain't," Miguel said. "And your uncle knows what he's talking about. So he must have meant the other way."

I sighed. I felt like yelling at him, but I had no good reason. Maybe I was just angry he made such a big deal about the Palabok Bandero, which, I admit, wasn't half-bad. Maybe it was something else. I wasn't hurting, but a tense itch permeated through my body, and it was signaling worse times ahead unless I took my medication. And maybe he was right. What the hell did I know?

We kept driving. Arthur Street, turned right onto Hayes, but our directions said Arthur turned onto Garfield which turned onto Hayes. We kept driving in circles past low-slung houses looking small but expensive, twisting slow and wide streets with signs letting us know children were at play. A car passed us rarely, sometimes an SUV and sometimes an old pickup truck. One lawn was covered in toys and playpens, but I saw no children about, or even heard them. Some 'For-Sale' signs hung at odd angles, weeds growing up around them.

I glanced up at the broad, blue sky. A solitary bird soared in spirals above.

"Hank. Look at the trees," Miguel said.

"What?" I squinted around.

"The lichen covers some of them. It's weird."

"Yeah." I'd registered it before, but didn't put a lot of thought into it. I was looking around for people. Or something. "Look, that one over there doesn't have any."

"It's a cedar," Miguel said. But he slowed down.

"A what?" I asked.

"A cedar. An evergreen. The lichen trees are all deciduous."

I frowned. I guessed he meant non-evergreen, like oaks or elms. Weren't elms even really trees, just large bushes? I'd heard that somewhere. God damn, the itch bothered me. It wasn't even really an itch, just a sense of feeling ill at ease with my own body. I didn't want to get the meaning of deciduous from Miguel, it'd seem too . . . it'd make me feel stupid around him. But I could already feel his scorn, and it was starting to bother me.

Fuck, I could just share some of the painkillers with him, and take some now to ease the discomfort, but then he might not be good enough to drive. Where the hell was Garfield? I wanted a lazy orange cat whose thoughts were easily dismissed. The street seemed to be in some arcane place maps failed to show, or didn't want to. Damn California and its pre-fab towns. Damn sub-developments like this and everywhere, all the same, paper houses and paper lawns, all in some bland synchronicity. No matter what town it was, they all went to the same chain restaurants. Took glee in the new menu additions, took drinks from the same twenty-something disaffected bartenders. Went home and relentlessly rode nowhere in stationary bikes all bought at the same Wal-Mart, just in different places all over the country. There was nothing new about America but the climate.

"This is starting to creep me out," Miguel said. "And it's getting dark. As your attorney, I advise you to get that hotel back the way we came and hole up for the night, with enough booze and drugs to forget about this little shithole." He wasn't my attorney. I forgot where he got the reference from, but he was awful fond of it. He smiled. "And I know you got drugs, Hank."

I made a bitter face. "The house is just around the way. Maybe you should double back. You keep driving too quickly. We must have missed a sign."

"I'm keeping the speed limit. Your uncle's brother-in-law just lives in a shitty location, that's all." Miguel's eyes widened. "What if we find them dead in the house? What if their hungry ghosts come looking for us? This fucking town creeps me out, man. Too many dead things. It's haunted."

"I said it was . . . oh, never mind." My shoulders slumped.

"What if this town's built over some Indian burial ground?" Miguel asked.

I shook my head. "That ain't happening."

"You don't know that, man."

"I do, though." I frowned. "If this town is built over an Indian burial ground, it's only because the fucking country was. I read that millions of Indians died of smallpox before even the first real settlement in the US took off. Whole cultures wiped out in a generation. The ghosts were there, waiting, when the country got founded. They've always been with us, so why the hell would they care about one little town?"

"Because, it's, like, a mystic site or something."

"That's just bullshit." I could barely get the words out. I was tired as hell, and every street looked the same. Where was home, here? Had it ever existed? Had I imagined talking to my uncle? Had I made us drive all the way down to this God-forsaken suburban town because of some dream? I shifted and glanced at Miguel. He was fiddling with the radio, his mind already on some other tangent.

We drove, turning left onto Pierce Street. Miguel fiddled with the radio and then turned it off. A great silence descended upon us, broken only by the wind outside and the apologetic cough from the engine of Miguel's car.

Miguel glanced at me out of the corner of his eye. "You got any of that prescription stuff? You brought it with you?"

I made a face. I could feel myself stiffening. That little slimeball. Trying to guilt his way into stuff I need, stuff the doctor gave me. But I knew it was silly of me to feel that way. And he was my only ride back. "Yeah," I croaked.

Miguel grinned to himself and kept driving, humming some soft and cheerful tune.

❖

Miguel spat. "That ain't a street! It's like an alley at best!"

"It's a cul-de-sac," I said, tonelessly. **GARFIELD ST.** was white letters on a thin line of green metal. The street had maybe four houses. I felt sad for the street somehow. Where could it have gone, where could it have meandered if it had only been given a chance? Instead it sat, hopeless and forgotten. My cousin-in-law was house #3. No car in the driveway. I scanned the others, saw an old Dodge in one drive, but otherwise empty.

"Can't tell if anyone's in any of the other houses," Miguel mumbled. "Maybe we should knock on doors."

"Let's wait," I said. "I'd feel weird having to explain myself." And I wanted to not be in a car anymore. Not be around people if I could manage it. I wanted to be at peace.

"Good idea," Miguel said. He parked in the driveway and we got out. We ambled up to the front door. Mail was stuffed into the mail slot. Miguel eyed it and looked at me. I shrugged, and knocked on the door.

No answer. I knocked again. Miguel tapped his foot, which somehow made me feel even more antsy. Everything about this town smelled bad. We really should've just left. But you haven't been there. Once you drive far enough, all you want to do is get something out of the journey. It doesn't feel fair.

"More lichen on the trees," Miguel mumbled.

I knocked one last time, then fished through my pocket and got the keys my uncle gave me. With some fiddling, the door opened. I pulled the mail out and walked in.

Inside looked like a wreck of a museum made for people to mock seventies living: shag carpets, modular couches, a sunken den-like living room with wood siding, glass sliding doors. Miguel tip-toed in deferentially. I slumped in and crashed on the couch.

"I'm gonna look for bodies," Miguel said.

I nodded to him and glanced down at the mail. I picked through it and sniffed. Shouldn't bodies stink up the place? I shook my head.

The last piece of mail was dated ten days ago. It was from a bank. Some tiny bit of morality nagged just as I was about to open it, but I overcame that quick and ripped the envelope.

The foreclosure statement seemed dry and bland. What a shame, something that could change your life would look so boring and lifeless. You wanted that kind of thing served by men who twirled mustaches and cackled dark and low. Men who wore effeminate capes, that sort of shit. Instead of vague, unappealing numbers, facts and figures and legal statements.

There was lots of other private and confidential mail. I was guessing the unmarked ones were credit card statements. The massive majority were credit card offers. Shit that said confidential so you'd open the letter and read about the incredibly low introductory rate, instead of just tossing it aside.

"Nothing," Miguel said, returning and slumping into the reclining chair, which looked a little like he was being consumed by pillows. "I think we're free on the body department, but I didn't spend too much time in the basement."

"This place has a basement?" I asked. "Shit, these houses usually don't."

Miguel's shrug was lazy and effortless. "What can I say?" He said. "They do shit old school down here in San Agosto."

There was a sudden noise. Miguel looked like he was about to jump out of his skin. We exchanged all sorts of vague looks at one another. I got up and we crept back to the kitchen.

Through the glass sliding door, we saw a pack of dogs filing through the weed-strewn yard. Maybe five or six, of all kinds of breeds. They seemed bedraggled, skinny, their fur matted and nicked. All different varieties. A collie, a sad-looking golden retriever, you name it. One gazed on me, his eyes glittering doll-like. It seemed unnatural. Un-dog-like. I tapped on the glass and the rest looked up as one, ears swiveling forward. Then one bolted, and the rest followed. I realized I was holding my breath.

Miguel said, “Whoa.”

I opened the sliding door and stepped out into the yard. “All these weeds, feels like people have been gone longer than ten days, don’t you think?”

Miguel said, without affect, “Dunno.”

I glanced back. “You’re the expert on this stuff.” But he just shrugged.

The yard was out of sorts. Someone had cut half the lawn and stopped, leaving the mower out there. A high fence blocked the view of the neighbors’ lawns, but I could see the hole the pack of animals had gone through. I squinted at the trees. “Whoa,” I said.

“What?” Miguel’s voice sounded absent and a little nervous.

“The trees, look.” I pointed. Dark reddish sap dripped from the trunks. “They’re bleeding.”

“Sudden Oak Death,” Miguel said.

“What?”

"It's a blight. Hit Northern California pretty bad. Not supposed to be this far south. Just kills off all the trees, acres at a time. They don't have a cure. It just wipes them out." His voice was sad and lost.

"Even the cedars?" I asked, turning back to him, trying to grin.

"No," Miguel said. "No evergreens." His look was sour. He wanted no joking. We went back inside.

❖

After that, we puttered around for a while and went to give Uncle a call, but neither one of us had coverage. I convinced Miguel to head back up the road, grab us some beer, call my uncle.

Miguel squinted at me. "If I come back and find your desiccated corpse, or like, you ain't here, I'm just gonna leave, okay?"

"Okay," I said. It seemed fair.

The moment he left, I dry-swallowed two pills and fumbled to the fridge to choke it down. Then I had another, just because I felt spooked. I sat in the middle of the couch staring at the blank TV, feeling miserable. The money hadn't been worth it. I know my uncle just wanted to give me a bit of extra money but make me feel like I was working it off, but it still felt weird to me. Too easy, too much like a handout. I had nothing going

on in my life. Girl had left six months ago. What
now? I was adrift. I didn't want it to be like this, but
figure out any other way.

This whole thing had gotten too complicated. Where was I now? What if Miguel never came back? I'd just be stuck here, in the middle of this weird suburban wasteland. I met my cousin-in-law once at one of my uncle's things. He seemed nice. A balding guy, he kept his hair cut short against his skull. Wore an old tee shirt with some band's name on the front. Khaki pants that fit, black shoes. My uncle and him talked about some fucking grill for the better part of an hour while I nursed a beer, my thoughts circling over and over again about some girl that wasn't even at the party. His wife was some Chinese chick, older than him, snippy and almost unconsciously hostile to everyone else at the party, including me, but I didn't care. When their eyes met, they both got this soft smile at each other.

I think the last I heard she was pregnant or something, and then the accident happened and I kind of lost touch with what was going on with the family for a while.

I knew the drug hitting me because my hand felt heavy, wonderfully heavy, and an immense calm fell over me like the nicest blanket in the world. My face and skin felt cold, but it was a good cold, a really happy cold. I was good in my skin, I didn't care who knew it. I knew I was smiling. It felt a little silly to be smiling, but I was going to anyways.

I laid back and stared at the ceiling for a while, then clicked on the TV and surfed through channel after channel of pleasant static. I kept thinking I saw figures there, moving like soldiers creeping up to the front in the middle of a blizzard, but I couldn't make out anything but muffled noises under the huuuuush of the tv. The figures were going to go where they had to go, I just didn't have the place to see them right. That was okay, I didn't need to worry. And Miguel would be back with beer. I wondered who the figures in the static were. The head of one of them occasionally talked to me in some far-off voice. Some ghostly commentator? Maybe it was a sports program or some kind of reality show. All that time and effort, all those production values to talk to me and I couldn't hear a damned thing they were saying. But then I heard something else.

I turned the TV off. You hear something quick, you can't remember what you hear because you weren't paying attention—there's just this sensation like you should have heard it, like it was somehow important.

I felt every tiny piece of skin I had. I heard the slow movements of air in the house. I saw how still the air was. No sound.

An age of indecision passed, and I got up. Prowled back to the kitchen. Checked the garage. Looked upstairs—an office, a master bedroom, a kid's room but it had a sewing machine set up and the cradle piled with shirts and old magazines. Nothing. Was it a cat outside, maybe? Those dogs back again?

I stood perfectly still on the upstairs landing and waited for the sound. Nothing.

There. Maybe. Downstairs? I didn't know. In a horror movie I would have been screaming at the television set to not go downstairs. Slasher movies were a game you knew people were going to lose. In a slasher movie you don't investigate the darkened place—that's where the bad people are. You waited for attractive people to make out, punishing the curious, living for shock, waited for the one conservative, virtuous, white-clad woman to step in and take the enemy down.

In real life, you investigated the unknown, so you can fucking go to sleep at night. You think: no, that's not an ogre in the darkness. That's not some creepy thing my grandmother would hoarsely whisper at me. It's just the fucking cat.

Miguel had said he hadn't spent much time in the basement. He'd *pointed that out.*

I couldn't believe it myself, but I crept down to the basement. Step by creaking step. It was tiny. More like a bomb shelter than anything else. Maybe that's what it was made for. The light didn't work. Figures. Miguel sure was taking his time getting back.

My hands were slow and thick catching the light fixture up and down, fiddling with it. I took deep breaths because it felt so wonderful to take them. I still felt anxious, but the anxiety was softened by cotton balls and lemon-scented ready-wipes. I was impervious and clean. And the slasher wasn't in the basement.

They stored the stupidest shit down here. I wanted a kiddy-porn dungeon. Or a ghost. Fucking *something*, man.

❖

An hour. Maybe two. I wasn't sure of the time. All of the clocks were blinking 12:00, but my phone had what I had to assume was the right time—only I never checked when Miguel left for beer in the first place. Maybe he got chicken and high-tailed it out. Who knows? It was getting late. He'd find me. I could crash out here.

My face felt heavy and slow. Sleep wanted to be with me, love me, brush the hair from my eyes and whisper soothing things in my ear. I thought I'd let it, but stumbled upstairs. They had a nice bed up there.

I woke to another one of those sounds you don't remember enough to know what the sound was. I was tangled in the bed. So soft and warm. Then I heard something again, a clump, maybe a voice. I couldn't tell.

Miguel? How long had I been out, anyways? Could I trust that was him?

The room was agonizingly dark. If I remembered correctly, there was a broom out in the hallway to the stairs. I crept out of bed and headed out, picking up the stick. Heard muttering downstairs, but couldn't make out the words. Something soft. Maybe the original family had returned. Or their ghosts, prowling downstairs listlessly and sad. I swallowed, and crept down the stairs. I hoped the staircase didn't creak. It didn't.

I saw a shadow at the bottom of the stairs and thought, *Ghost*. Before I could run, I heard myself call out in a commanding voice, "Hey!"

The shadow squeaked most unspectrally. "Who is it?"

"What're you doing here?"

I heard another voice. "What the fuck is that?" it seemed to say, rushing in. "We're not alone, I don't think—oh my god! Someone else! I'm so sorry! We'll get right out of here."

"No. Stop. What's happening here?" I asked, holding the broom threateningly. I could see the shadows shifting. A girl and a guy, maybe. A guy and another guy who happened to have a higher-pitched voice. I didn't know. I held the broom like a gun.

"You don't know?" the deeper voice asked.

"I just got here," I said.

"You don't live here?" the squeakier voice asked.

"I got back from vacation. Look. What the fuck? Just tell me. What happened to all the people? Where did they all go?"

"We don't know, man. I come from the town down the road. Heard from a friend the other day. No one really knows. I don't see anything on the news or nothing."

The softer voice said: "My cousin, he was in this bar, said a guy came in from up north. Heading to Mexico. Said he had a friend in the town next to him, just upped and vanished. His wife's sister stopped answering her phone from her farm north of Ukiah. They just assumed the worst. Bank took the house back, anyways. They just said, 'Fuck it,' and left."

"That's bullshit," I said. "What about the cops?"

"I ain't heard nothing," said the male voice.

The female voice snorted, her shadowy form shifting. "Like they even care," she whispered low.

"Hey," said the guy. "Is that even a gun?"

I tensed. Just then, headlights from a car plied across the room, I saw the figure of the guy—just a silhouette, all darkness, and the girl. Her dark hair in her face. Eyes glittering strangely, like the dog I had seen before.

"The cops?" one said. There was cursing.

"You wait here!" I said. I don't even know why. I made a move, there were sparks first and then a loud crack, like thunder. My leg gave out even before the pain shot through it, and I tumbled down the stairs. Pain encased me, like a friend returning from abroad.

I don't know how much time had passed, but Miguel was there. He kept asking me, "*What the fuck happened to you? What the hell did you do to your leg?*" But I wanted none of that. I was sad. I couldn't be anything else but sad.

"We gotta find out what became of them, Miguel! We gotta stay and figure this out," I croaked.

"No," Miguel said calmly. "We don't gotta do any of that. You're hurt. We're going."

"We gotta figure this out! This shit happens . . . " I felt a dull throb of pain from my leg. When I put weight on it, it stung. My pants were cold and wet and sticky. "It happens for a reason. There has to be a moral." There has to be a moral, because if there wasn't, what does that mean to us? Who are we, then?

"You're hurt, Hank. Can you make it a little further? The car's just that way."

My shrug was a faint vibration; the solitary flap of a hummingbird's wings.

He pulled my arm around his neck. He chuckled. "You know, at least you got something for the pain."

"We can't leave them here, Miguel!" I cried.

"Who?" He said.

"All them ghosts." I don't know what I was saying. I felt impossibly sad. All those houses. All those families. Just gone, and nobody knew and nobody cared. Was that the way of life? Was that our purpose? Just to be flushed out with the flick of some divine wrist? How many times had this happened in the world? I thought of all those people talking about outdoor grills and looking forward to Tuesday nights and the televised singing competitions, just snuffed out. "It hurts," I said.

"I know," Miguel said. "Just a little further."

He slid me into the passenger seat and lit a cigarette, then slid in the driver's seat and turned over the engine. The lights flickered on and the engine coughed. I saw something in the shadows there: the pack of dogs, maybe more of them. Hunched figures, ears swiveled forward. Eyes shining, eyes watching. Always watching. Always hungry, always waiting.

I don't know if he saw them. He gunned the engine. He was sweating—had he helped himself to my stash before, and I hadn't noticed? Or was he scared? I felt delirious, I wished I could tell.

The car crept away. I turned and thought of my uncle's brother-in-law, rubbing his head, smiling dumbly. The polo shirt, the expression on his face. I tried to fix it in my memory, but I couldn't see his face. We pulled off the street and I watched it fade away, illuminated only by the taillights of Miguel's car: dark looming shadows with hints of red, fading into nothing.

WHAT PRESIDENT POLK SAID

Vylar Kaftan

You have to understand how it was. No doctors. No hospitals. Most of us hadn't seen civilization in months. Years, if you counted the fellows who camped here last winter instead of heading to Sacramento. We each had a pick—most of us—and boots, and clothes, and dreams. We were covered in mud and never came clean. That's what we shared, all of us 'Niners.

And Dawson was crazy as a loon. Bigger than any man I'd ever seen: near seven foot tall and broad as a wagon's backside. His breeches fit like leggings and his flannel exposed his elbows. We all smelled worse than a dog's behind, but Dawson stank like a festering wound. He harassed everyone in the camp—white, Negro, or Mexican. He pushed up at night into a man's face like a desperate whore: "Where's the gold? Did you find gold?"

Dawson knew the truth, he said. The government planted the gold out here to tempt greedy men. The Army was waiting to see who died. They'd round up the survivors and sell them to the Injuns. When he spoke like this, he got a terrible gleam in his eye, and you knew all sense had left the man. Dawson muttered to his Bowie knife at night, calling it President Polk. He'd sneak up on men, grab them by the neck, and bring out the knife. "President's coming for you, boys." Scared the greenhorns out of their wits, but he always let them go.

Dawson was held to be scary but harmless. But when someone stole Kingsley's gold right out from his tent, we knew it was Dawson. Axman Joe said he saw Dawson skulking round the tent, like he was going to piss but changed his mind. We trusted Joe. Everyone knew everyone's business here. We all knew where each man slept and how he scratched himself. We knew who the thieves were and they weren't us. That's how we got through the days: trusting each other, because if we didn't we'd start killing each other. Words were whispered, opinions exchanged, and some of us decided to meet by the old tree north of camp.

The tree was like Dawson—a broad oak, taller than its fellows. It was bent in the middle like it had battled another tree for the right to grow. That tree was older than California, a century perhaps, while this state was only two years old. Perhaps the tree was insane as well; I couldn't tell with trees.

There were four of us—me, the Crane brothers, and Axman Joe. The Crane brothers just wanted him gone. It was Joe who said we had to take it further. Joe said a gold thief would be slitting throats in a week. "Saw it in Stockton," he said, fingering his knife.

And there it was. Couldn't kill him. Couldn't let him go. We knew what happened to murderers—hanging. But we also couldn't let him steal gold from other camps. That's what I'm telling you: we had to trust each other to get through the days. That meant everyone, including men at other camps.

We hatched a plan. Joe was a burly guy, ex-coal miner. The brothers were farm boys, strong as oxen. That left me, the educated man, to do the persuading. My weapon was whiskey. I spent my last gold on the best bottle I could get. I whispered my plan to Dawson. We'd meet at the old oak on Sunday afternoon, just him and me, and get sopping drunk. His eyes widened and I knew I had him.

When the time came, Axman Joe and the Crane brothers crouched behind a rock. I sat under the tree with the whiskey. Dawson came up the hill, with President Polk tucked in his belt like always. He and I drank together. He did most of the talking. He ranted about suspenders and Chicago and the Army's plans for us all. The sun crept across the sky. We got drunker. He drank more, but he was bigger. It seemed like he'd never go down.

Suddenly a twig snapped nearby. Dawson stopped mid-sentence and tilted his head. I feared the worst. He said, "Listen."

I did. I was so drunk I could hardly think. Birds chirped and a stream was running in the distance. I thought I heard someone moving behind the rock. Dawson whispered, "President Polk wants to talk to you."

The trees spun around me. The knife. I thought I was supposed to be doing something about the knife. That was the plan. "All right," I said, wondering if he meant he would kill me.

Dawson nodded gravely. "Listen closely," he said. He handed

me the knife. I fumbled blindly before taking it. I heard the blood rushing through my ears like the American River. My pan was coming up empty. I held the knife to my ear, listening for gold nuggets.

Well, the other three took that as their cue. They jumped him. Dawson was a mean drunk, but a stupid one, and he'd had enough to miss his punches. I ducked out of the way. The three of them overpowered him. They drove him to the ground and bound his wrists and legs.

We strapped him to that oak, tight enough to hold but not constrict him. He howled like a demon. He kicked and screamed, and then got hysterical and soiled himself. We backed away slowly, mumbling promises about bringing him food. We didn't think we'd keep them.

We went back to the camp. The others wondered where he'd gone, but not for long. Men came in and out of camps all the time. If anyone guessed the truth, they must have approved. Dawson became a camp legend told to scare greenhorns. I kept his knife. One Bowie looks just like another, and no one realized it was President Polk.

Four days later I struck the motherlode—gold like a waterfall dried in place on the rock wall. I dug my fortune, gave away my pick, and got the hell out of there. I still have the knife.

I see that look. You're thinking I went back to the tree. Well, I thought about it. Thing was, I couldn't do it. I know what he'd want. But by God, the preachers say we'd go to hell for murder. You have to understand. There was nothing else we could do.

Every summer, I get President Polk from his hiding place in my bureau. And I say, "You see how it was, don't you?" All these years, the knife's never spoken to me. I wish it would. If President Polk explained himself, I'd know I was mad. And that would excuse the thing we did that afternoon.

KINDER

Steve Berman

Alexander sniffed the damaged book. *The Brim Above the Brow: Meditations on the Chapeau.* His nose caught a blend of must from the foxed pages and an unexpected sweetness. He ran a fingertip along the scalloped edges of the bite mark. Strong jaws but the teeth had to be small. Perhaps a rat? The thought disgusted him. He peered at the bookcase and moved aside the 1902 edition of *Lexicon of European Millinery* and *The Proper Tip: Social Demands of the Bowler.* No droppings, no debris, only the usual dust that Ms. Penn attacked once a week.

He crouched down on his knees. The titles on the lowest shelf were novels and collections. Early editions rendered near worthless by cracked spines and loose pages. Every so often, a Trustee would present a plan to sell one. Had the rats disliked Hawthorne? He pulled out his note pad and scribbled a reminder to ask Mr. Cassey to bring his poisons early this season.

For the next few hours, Alexander searched the rest of the study for any other damage or misplaced objects. He found the remains of a lollipop underneath Grueller's mahogany desk. Wine-colored sugar crystals clung to the worn Persian rug.

"Children," Alexander muttered to the empty room.

He wore gardening gloves while removing the offending stick. Alexander had heard somewhere that a dog's mouth was cleaner than a child's. He imagined both as drooling pits.

He had asked the Board on several occasions during his years as caretaker that Grueller House not admit any person under ten years of age, no matter how many adults were present. How could a child appreciate the historical worth of Pennsylvania's—arguably the entire Eastern seaboard's—preeminent late 19th century hatter? Bored tourists stumbled upon the sidewalk sign were bad enough. Alexander shuddered whenever someone other than the quiet graduate students or powdered, old women from the Historical Society came through the front door.

After one last walk through the house, Alexander turned off the lights and headed upstairs, his feet avoiding the bald patches on the runner. He went through the second floor hall, with its thirteen coat racks capped with russet derbies, tan fedoras, and homburgs of dusty silver felt. Past the master bedroom, Grueller's changing area had been refurbished for the caretaker's stay. Crème-colored walls held the early summer's heat, and Alexander stripped down entirely before slipping into bed. He closed his eyes and listened to the house groan.

❖

Standing before the hallway mirror, Alexander adjusted the hat, which resembled a pale thimble ornamented with a white satin band and silver buckle. He hid the price tag. The gift shop offered replicas of Grueller designs. Boxes from China filled the basement.

He checked his watch: just shy of 10 A.M. and he still had several chores and piles of paperwork unattended. When Henry had been docent, there had been time for everything.

Alexander unlocked the front door.

In the late afternoon, the first visitor arrived: an elderly woman in a bold floral dress smelling of rose water. She tilted her head back and forth while looking around the foyer. "Did anyone die here? Someone important. I'm a mystery writer, you know." She took a gilded pen and small memo pad from her canvas bag. "I'm doing research. I just adore cozies."

"The only cozies used at Grueller House are found in the dining room."

The woman nodded and began scribbling. Her bag toppled the stack of slick brochures on the demilune table.

Alexander bent down to recover the brochures when the children stampeded past him. An arm smacked the side of his face, and fingers scratched his cheek. Wincing, he checked his face in the mirror. His reflection scowled as he touched the edges of the red marks underneath one eye.

"You should keep those children on a leash." He did not see where they went but heard them running through the house's first floor.

"They aren't my children." She finished whatever notes

she'd been making and headed off, not in the direction of the dining room, clearly marked, but the parlor.

Alexander tracked the sounds of gaiety and stomping feet to the front room. A boy in lederhosen and a girl in a blouse and Bavarian skirt ran around a table set with Grueller's tools. They must have come straight from some school play. The Heidi reached for the pair of calipers used to measure the skull, not touched since a tipsy Henry had used them as ice tongs.

"Stop that." Alexander clapped his hands to get their attention. "This is not a playroom. Where are your parents?" He hated how shrill his voice became around children.

The pair stopped on the other side of the table. Spittle filled the edges of the boy's toothy smile and dribbled down to his dimpled chin. The little Heimlich fell to all fours and bit at the 19th century mahogany. Wood crunched and splinters clung to his lips.

Alexander shouted in astonishment and kicked at the kid. Its belly felt oddly solid, enough to hurt his toes. The Heimlich rolled and struck a chair. A plump hand reached up to the chair's seat.

"That's priceless. Off, off!" Although Alexander knew the chair wasn't an authentic Chippendale but a weak reproduction limited by the unimaginative splat.

The Heimlich nodded and started gnawing at a leg. Heidi came over with a mouthful of feathers. She clutched a deflated down pillow.

"Get out! Out, out, now." He grabbed them by their ears and pulled them towards the door. They snarled in some Alpine tongue. "No unattended children at Grueller House." He hoped they did not belong to one of the Trustees, the majority of whom were laywers.

The pair stared at him from the sidewalk a moment. Then the Heidi bent down to nibble on the step's wrought-iron railing. Heimlich scratched his pudgy head and yawned, showing a mouthful of endless teeth leading to a very red gullet.

He slammed the door shut and turned the deadbolt. He leaned against the wood while he caught his breath. He'd call for Mr. Cassey and demand he spray tomorrow. Then he'd have to speak to someone at Winterthur about restoration. And the Trustees would have to be involved.

Scrolling through the long list of contacts on his cell phone, Alexander paused at Henry's name.

They had not spoken in the weeks since the Trustees had dismissed Henry. If not for a forthcoming article on Grueller in the *Journal of the History of Ideas*, Alexander might have also been let go. The gratitude at being given a second chance turned to shame whenever he thought of calling Henry.

At night, Alexander found he couldn't ignore the house. The walls felt brittle, the rooms no longer had a sense of refinement and seclusion but left him anxious. He missed Henry's soft voice, the way his snores sounded more like repeated sighs.

In the kitchen he was horrified to find the large woman who wanted cozies with her head in the Oberlin stove, one of the few surviving in Pennsylvania. Murmurs of regret over failing to bring a tape measure echoed in the oven. Her dress had caught on the oven's lower ledge to expose a glossy lavender-shaded slip and legs covered with ruddy blotches.

"Madam," Alexander said with a gasp. He imagined a swift

kick to her posterior but that might wedge her tight. "Remove yourself from the Oberlin." He was relieved that cast iron resisted scratching.

She scuttled back and blinked at him for a moment. "Just as well. They're all convection these days." She made further notations before rising to her feet.

After escorting her back to the foyer, he unlocked the door for her. He took notice that she paused by the bronze box for donations bolted to one wall. She even lifted the swinging lid and peered inside.

He took a firm hold of her arm and guided her to the door. "We have no mysteries here."

❖

Caretakers were not permitted to cook their meals on the Oberlin. Not that Alexander had known the urge to chop wood. In the back utility room, he heated a can of *Krimmel's Old Pepper Pot Stew* over a portable electric burner. He stabbed apart a congealed lump, suspected of being tripe.

Around him, Grueller House groaned. Alexander paused in his stirring and listened. Strong winds would turn the plaster walls into a bellows. He wondered if the house found comfort in creaking. Then he heard laughter.

He went into the hallway. Most of the house was dark. Something short dashed from one room to the next. Giggles and grunts trailed behind it. Floorboards creaked beneath Alexander's argyles.

He could hear the sound of their chewing, a cacophony of

rippling cloth, breaking wood, and cracking glass. Their lips smacked. Mastication. Gulps as they swallowed.

He turned on the parlor's lights. Heimlich and Heidi looked up from where they sat on the floor, the remnants of the furniture on their wet cheeks and chins. Their wide eyes had tiny blue dots in the center.

The pair retreated behind the curtain, their fat bellies bulging the muslin. Thick fingers clutched the fabric's edge. Four shiny patent leather shoes gleamed at the bottom.

"I'm calling the cops," Alexander said as he walked over to them. "They'll take you to dank cells where rough men pee in corners!"

He pulled aside the curtains and found the shoes were empty. Without arms, without hands, the fingers toppled to the floor like weisswurst, sickly pale and wrinkled at the knuckles.

Alexander didn't call the police. His hands shook as he opened the bottle of Wasmund's Single Malt, he'd bought days ago as an apology to Henry. The first sip of whiskey went straight to his sinuses. He only realized he'd left the burner on when he wandered to the back of the house and smelled burnt stew and pot, an acrid combination. He finished off the single malt as his dinner.

❖

Mr. Cassey arrived the next day as Alexander catalogued the damage. The exterminator's navy uniform had a patch on the front (*Francis*) and a silhouette of people standing around an immense, upturned beetle on the backside. Mr. Cassey smelled like cigarette smoke; he had once told Alexander that only the two packs a day habit protected his lungs from the toxins he used.

"So, any more rat sightings? They're a colony. Not a swarm."

"No, I think it's German children." Alexander suspected that the house's insurance policy might not cover such damage.

"Oh, then it's a hamlin of kinder. Very dangerous. Are they Weimar or Nazi?"

"They're German, isn't that bad enough?" Alexander blinked. For a moment, Mr. Cassey's name patch had read *Franz.* "Um, they might be Alpine."

Mr. Cassey nodded. Then he tore the cellophane off a new pack, shoving the crackling wad into a pocket. He went back into his van and came out with a lit cigarette and a metal canister.

Alexander took several steps back. He didn't know how flammable Mr. Cassey might be. "Why are these kinder here?"

A puff of blue-gray smoke emerged from Mr. Cassey's mouth as he scratched an armpit. "Normally happens in winter. They're drawn by the smell of lonely folk."

With the aid of his handkerchief, Alexander waved aside the smoke. "I'm not lonely."

"Witches. Bitches. Bachelors." Mr. Cassey smirked, which bent the cigarette. "Especially life-long bachelors."

Alexander felt his face flush. "My mother endeavored for years to convey the lofty wisdom she gleaned from her subscription to *Redbook,* Mr. Cassey. She failed to straighten me out," he said while stiffening his back.

Mr. Cassey dropped the cigarette on the street and slipped on an old World War II-era gas mask. The round lenses reflected the world askew; Alexander could not see the face beneath the dark rubber. He had a strange feeling that Mr. Cassey was choosing to reveal his true, insectile face. His voice buzzed. Whatever he said to Alexander while entering the house was incomprehensible.

Alexander remained on the sidewalk. It drizzled slightly, possibly ruining the fez he wore. He wished he had a paperback or sudoku or something to waste the time. He considered heading over to browse the shop windows on Antique's Row.

When the front door opened again, wisps of vapor announced Mr. Cassey's exit. He doffed the mask. "That should take care of them. I also sprayed for enfants."

Once inside, Alexander found several kinder lying on their backs with limbs close and crooked to their torsos. Each golden-haired Heimlich and Heidi looked exactly alike, down to their rosy cheeks, fading to gray, and swollen tongues poking through dark lips.

It took Alexander a long time to bag all the children. He filled both trashcans and afterwards had legs poking out beneath he lids. He was sure the garbage men would give him grief over taking them.

"Being single is not a crime," he muttered as he dialed Henry's number.

❖

Alexander thanked Henry for holding the bag of takeout so he could find his keys. Worry made him turn the front door knob too hard. Would he find the foyer a disaster? Gnawed ribs of the staircase banisters, wallpaper peeled like the skin of some fruit, and Teutonic tittering in the air?

He sighed and patted his chest in relief when greeted by welcome tidiness.

He walked over to the nearest hat rack and lifted off a Stetson. "Your fav—"

"I think I'll stick with this," Henry said and nudged the brim of a garish crimson and white baseball cap.

"Oh." Alexander attempted a smile.

Henry shook his head. "I suppose knowing the Phillies are one of the oldest baseball teams won't help." He lifted off the cap. The sparse hair beneath was matted.

"It's fine." Alexander patted Henry's beefy forearm. "Let's eat."

He had made sure to spread a tablecloth over the small card table. He took out from the bag a wedge of Saga Blue. The woman at the cheese shop had promised it was Danish, thus safer than Cambozola, but Alexander eyed its mottling warily.

He asked Henry to get a long knife from a drawer to cut the bread, then looked around to see Henry was gone. A staccato of clinks came from the old house.

Alexander rushed to the dining room. He expected *kinder,* not Henry removing china from the breakfront. "We shouldn't," he said.

"Don't say these were Grueller's." Henry tipped the plate he held against his chest. The gilded rim was worn in spot. "A Trustee's wife donated the set when she redecorated her Rittenhouse Square apartment."

"I know." Alexander sighed.

Henry set the plate down on the long table. "Did we ever get caught? When we came back from *Giselle*—"

"Your first ballet." Alexander had begged one of the Trustees to secure him excellent seats.

"My first."

"And the first time I ever lit the fireplace." Alexander closed the breakfront.

"After two bottles of wine." Henry laughed. He touched Alexander's cheek with his thick hand. The callus on his thumb scratched at the tapered ends of Alexander's mustache. "Nothing happened. Not to the andirons, not to the screen."

"The chinoiserie screen," Alexander whispered. It had such a lovely image of white pebbles spaced along a lonely path leading to a sweet cottage. His eyes closed as he leaned into Henry's palm. He was aware of the slouch of his own spine, the feel of blood carrying the warmth of that touch throughout his cheek, then face, before descending his neck to spread throughout torso and limbs. How could such a simple gesture weaken him so? "But the Trustees . . . "

"Tell them you want me here."

Alexander welcomed the onset of apprehension. "This is about your job?" He stepped back from Henry.

"No. I just thought . . . if I was docent again . . . " Henry brought up a finger to his mouth and worried the nail with his teeth.

"And the Trustees' disapproval for our . . . liaisons?" Alexander drew out the last word, turning each syllable to lead.

Henry shook his head. "The Trustees must pay extra for self-hating fags." He headed for the door.

The fixtures worked in Grueller's bathroom. Wearing the Stetson, Alexander treated himself to a bubble bath in the old claw foot tub, so massive it took nearly a half hour to fill. The scent of lavender and chamomile did not relieve the knots in his back or the hint of a migraine. The Godiva truffles he'd bought for dessert that night helped a little.

If only he understood the mystery of men as well as he did antiques. He shouldn't be lonely or ashamed of an affair with fellow staff. It was all such a nuisance compared to the task of having an entire house to worry over.

The doorknob rattled. A piece of chocolate dropped from Alexander's hand into the suds with a deep plop. The Stetson followed.

Sweet voices came from the other side of the door as fingers scratched the wood.

"Hier stehen die Manner vorm Spiegel stramm
Und schminken sich selig die Haut.
Hier hat man als Frau keinen Brautigam.
Hier hat jede Frau eine Braut."

Alexander heard chewing.

"Go away. I have a gun," he said, clutching the wet Stetson over his groin as he stood up in the tub.

The first kinder, a Heidi, broke through the thin wood. Half forced its way into the bathroom. One pigtail with a pink ribbon tied at the end dangled to the tiled floor. She gnashed the fragments left in her jaws. He felt her hungry stare.

"Good kinder." He held up the box of gold-wrapped chocolates. "Candy?"

The Heidi's round nose twitched. A stream of clear saliva dripped down its mouth.

"Delicious candy." Alexander slowly stepped out of the tub as the Heidi crawled through the hole in the door. A grinning Heimlich peered through after it.

Alexander threw a truffle at the Heidi's feet. It picked up the chocolate and smashed it against its lips, devouring the wrapper as well.

He let the hat fall and crushed it stepping back. He tossed another piece near the tub. The Heidi waddled over. The Heimlich already began eating the porcelain sink when it heard the Heidi grunting a sound that Alexander took for pleasure. The Heimlich fought to reach the next piece in time.

Plop! Alexander threw a chocolate into the full tub. Then the rest of the box. The kinder groped and fumbled up the slick slides before falling into the hot bath. They didn't seem to think about breathing as they dived for the sunken treats.

He pulled on his bathrobe. Two fat bodies began floating face down. The Heidi still clutched a melted truffle in one fist, and the chocolate leaked through the tight grip.

❖

Hanging the tin *Closed for Renovations* sign before noon the next day on the front door pained Alexander. Sundays brought the most visitors. But he could not permit even one patron to see him taking a hammer to one of the imitation Chippendale chairs, the one gnawed by kinder. Several times as he swung, the Stetson almost fell from his head.

Whenever his mother would end a whine with "Desperate times calling for desperate measures," Alexander would wince. Now, he found himself muttering the same as he struck that dreadful splat. It splintered with satisfaction.

Sacrifices, not measures, he told himself as he carried the kindling into the kitchen. One proved love through sacrifices. He had left Henry a message, begging him to come to the house for lunch. He had even admitted he'd be cooking for Henry on the Oberlin. After he'd hung up, he regretted leaving a recording of his crime.

Men must demand more than an understanding of historical significance. He fretted over so quickly abandoning his firm beliefs that any single individual paled in comparison to the worth of a hat on a rack or a rare cast-iron stove. He felt cooking this meal to be a bit of sedition, an impious act.

The Oberlin's hinges moaned when he opened the oven door. Alexander felt it appropriate to murmur gentle words to coax the oven back to life. "Such craftsmanship" and "Cold pans, warm hearth."

Deep in the back was the reservoir for wood. The gullet had

been empty for decades. He hoped the chimney worked and the smoke would rise.

In the back room, he took from the small refrigerator the makings for lunch. Alexander glanced at the cuckoo clock he'd moved from the kitchen after the first signs of kinder infestation. He kept meaning to check the old records to see if Grueller really did own a Bahnhäusle from the Black Forest. Now, he was more troubled that Henry was late by more than a half hour. He checked his cell phone, then the house phone, for messages but there were none. The kitchen grew warm as the wood burned.

He conceded that Henry would not come. Perhaps Henry despised him now. He expected a rush of sadness but could only summon up a mild measure of disappointment that threatened to become annoyance. He reasoned, as he laid the veal cutlets on a skillet, that Henry had only earned his heartache after being a constant at the Grueller House. When he had arrived wearing that . . . cap, he had been almost a different person.

As he lifted one lid from the stove with tongs, the oven trembled like a hound shedding water. That, and a clattering sound from behind him, made Alexander jump, dropping the skillet and lid with an even louder crash.

Flushed, he turned around. A Heimlich brought one glossy, patent leather shoe down hard on what remained of the tin sign—*for Ren.* It smacked its lips and advanced. Behind it, Heidis dashed from room to room.

With his back against the Oberlin—and he felt the heat through his trousers—Alexander stabbed with the tongs. The

Heimlich caught the curved ends in its pudgy fingers and wrenched the tool from his hands. The kinder began teething on the tongs. The Stetson dropped back and landed on the stovetop. The reek of charred felt filled the small kitchen.

"No," Alexander shouted. "I'm not lonely."

Something shoved him aside and he looked up from the floorboards to see the Oberlin stepping forward on its iron feet. The stump of chimney pipe had broke loose at the angle reminiscent a shark's fin. Its door and drawers slammed open and close like so many jaws with flickering tongues of fire.

The slightly burnt Stetson rolled off to land back on Alexander's scalp. The pan of veal landed at his feet.

The Heimlich tried to run but the Oberlin scooped the kinder inside it. Cries of German lasted only a moment. A new smell, sweet and rich like baked marzipan chased away the stink of singed felt. Despite his shock, Alexander found saliva filling his mouth.

The Oberlin kept shuffling, leaving the kitchen and entering the hallway. Alexander soon heard more Teutonic cries.

❖

Alexander began retiring to Grueller's bed at night. An indulgence. He'd rise early and make sure to change the bedding with fresh sheets and lay the quilt just right. Then, before opening, he'd let the Oberlin roam the house, on guard for kinder, before leading it back to the kitchen.

Enough lamp oil remained for him to proof his letter to the Trustees asking for an increase to the funds allocated to maintenance. He also adjusted his wording for the new docent ad he'd post tomorrow.

He leaned over the side of the high bed and patted the slumbering Oberlin's chimney stump. It wheezed from every crevice and the house echoed the sound, which Alexander decided must be contentment. Then he lifted off the cotton nightcap warming over the tea kettle atop the stove and went to sleep.

SET DOWN THIS

Lavie Tidhar

On my brother's computer, a video file shows an American fighter plane pinpointing a group of men in Iraq.

"Do it?" the pilot says.

"Confirmed."

"Ten seconds to impact."

Where the men have been there is a huge explosion, and black smoke covers the grainy grey streets. "Dude," the pilot says.

I have no faces and no names to put to the men. The black smoke must have contained the atoms of their flesh, their bones (though bones are hardy), vaporized sweat, burnt eyebrows and pubic hair and nose hair (unless they used a trimmer, as I do), in short, the atoms of their being. Later, I think, one could find, lying in the street, a tooth or two, the end of a finger that had somehow survived, fragments of bone, a legless shoe. These men are nothing to me. They are pixels on a screen, a peer-shared digital file uploaded from sources unknown, provenance suspect, whose only note of authenticity is that young pilot's voice when the smoke rises and he says, quietly— "Dude."

Let us pick a man at random from the video. His name is, let's say, Abu Karim. It means the father of Karim. He had given his son the name, perhaps, in honor of Kareem Abdul-Jabbar, because even men who die in targeted bombings might like basketball. He is five feet ten inches tall. You could say he is short, but he had never felt it. His son is taller than him, and he is proud of it. "My big son," he says. In Arabic the word is *jabar*. There is an Iraqi footballer, Haidar Abdul-Jabar Khadim, who plays for Jordan's Al-Wihdat club. He could have been named for the American basketball player, too.

We don't know what Abu Karim was doing on that street, with those others, at that time and at that place. Undoubtedly, the military minds behind the strike know, or at least suspect. Perhaps he is a terrorist, fighting the Americans who are trying to liberate Iraq. Perhaps he is a religious zealot, coming out of a radical madrassa with the other students. Perhaps he is a secular socialist, a former member of Saddam Hussein's Baath Party. It is impossible to tell from the video, and in any case his death does not concern us. It is, by its very existence, no longer in the bounds of right or wrong. It merely is.

Did the man have hobbies? Did he like to collect stamps, as pedestrian as that may seem? Did he covet the Cape Triangular, did he receive catalogs in the post from Stanley Gibbons, was his happiest secret moment his receipt of a mint Penny Black?

Poor countries produce stamps for collectors in more wealthy countries. Following the death of Saddam Hussein the Iraqi bank notes and stamps bearing his image were already selling at premium on London's Cecil Court.

I don't want to make him into a saint, though stamp-collectors are hardly that. Let's say Abu Karim is not a nice man. Whatever he was before—before the circumstances of his life changed—he is no longer that. He is, by implication of the bombing that had taken his life, a man guilty of a charge. Perhaps he killed. Perhaps this is not the first time he had escaped an attempt on his life. Another video on my brother's computer is called "The.Fastest.Man.in.Iraq." It is filmed from the point of view of a video-equipped guided bomb. It shows the target, and the approach, and in the same frame a man running inhumanly fast to get away before the bomb hits. It's a funny video. It is filed under Humor, next to Sports Bloopers, Animals and Children. I said he runs inhumanly fast, but now I think inhumanly is not the right word. He runs as fast as he (humanly) can. It could even be that he is Abu Karim, and that, that time, he survived. I don't know what he was before—a husband? A parent? A juice-seller or a preacher of the Koran or of Marxism?—but what had he become, and how? What led to his death, just or otherwise, and his digital re-birth as an extra in an Internet movie?

Of course I have no answers. Abu Karim is imaginary, after all. I can't shout after him, Jibel awiyah—bring your papers!—and expect him to present himself with ID and driving license and a passport one can no longer travel anywhere with. I cannot say—Wakef wa'ana batuchek—stop or I will shoot!—because he is both imaginary and, already dead. His ghost recedes away from me when I shout those things. When I try to ask him, nicely, to let me in, to ease my disquiet, when I say Iftach il-bab, ya khmar!—open the door, you donkey!—he won't answer, and the door to his mind, to his recall, remains closed to me. But more and more, since I had watched my brother's videos, I find myself in that state of this vague disquiet, and when I sleep I see his face, whole the way it was in life, staring at me with—but I can never tell, what that look in his eyes like black olives is.

The titles of my brother's videos are these:

Airplane F4-Crash
B52_crash
F14a_explosion (you can tell he is into flying)
F-16 in Falluja
F117_in_action
Hellfire_strike
Renegade platoon locates IED in Baquba February 2005

Roadside IED
Terrorist hunting-WARNING-abit-sick
Worst Kind of Ambush
. . . and so on.

Worst Kind of Ambush is another humorous video. We see a row of portable toilets. Two soldiers run at one of the cubicles, fell it down, and run away. The door opens to reveal a soldier with his pants down, holding a roll of toilet paper in one hand. "Nice ass!" a voice OC says.

IED stands for Improvised Explosive Device. It is the sort of charge Iraqi insurgents—those fighting the liberators of their country—set up by the side of the road, for instance—as, in fact, in the video labeled Roadside IED, and where the charge hits an American vehicle.

Did Abu Karim help build these IEDs? Did he kill American soldiers? Did he contribute, unknowingly, to more videos than the one featuring his last performance?

As a matter of fact, I suspect these videos do not exist. A Google search for "Terrorist hunting-WARNING-abit-sick" shows no results. The video, reminiscent of the screen of a computer game, shows figures running on the ground and an unnamed American pilot being directed to shoot first one, then another, and later blow up a truck with people inside it. It is unlikely such classified material would be made available on the Internet. Therefore I suspect it, too, is most likely propaganda: though I don't know whose.

❖

But back to Abu Karim. Or maybe not. Maybe go back, rather, to Karim. Is *he* dead? If not, is he too building IEDs?

More and more, Abu Karim invades my sleep, materializing in the black moments between sleep and awakening when I rise with a desperate need for the bathroom. He appears in the grogginess of early morning, before coffee and cigarettes banish him to the world of the dead again. He is my own private IED, improvised and explosive, with a son, a wife, a fruit-seller's job (as fanciful as that may be)—everything, in short, but a coffin. Why is he bothering me? It is possible, I suppose, that his atoms, blasted, were carried on the wind, like sand from the Sahara, half-way across the world, bringing him to me. It is possible I inadvertently inhaled them, it is even possible that my body, in its ceaseless quest of regenerating cells, had used some of those loose atoms to construct some minute part of my own body. Is that what is it? Is Abu Karim a cancer, trying to feed off of me? I want nothing of his. I want him to remain dead. I want him gone.

Bombattack
Bottle_head_shot
Die_terrorists_die
IED attack v Stryker
War_Footage_Iraqi_gets_LIT_UP

More recently the voice of Abu Karim has been growing faint, replaced with a voice I have no reason to believe is dead. I call him John. He sounds white, though I am not an expert on American accents. He usually says only one word. It is said with a kind of humorous awe.

Dude.

Did John go to college? Or did he go straight to the army at seventeen or eighteen? Somehow, he sounds to me like a college kid. Dude. Like when you drink beer through a hose, dude. It's called a beer bong. When you drink so much you get seriously bombed. Where did he come from? I know as much about Americans as I know about Iraqis, that is to say, very little. Can John be Karim's age? What movies does he like? What music? Is he a rock music guy? Does he prefer the constant beat of jungle? Who was his first girlfriend? When did he lose his virginity? Has he ever been to Vegas?

Different sets of questions, different assumptions. For all I know Abu Karim was never a fruit-seller. Perhaps he was a mechanical or chemical engineer. Perhaps he studied in America, before the war. It is possible, I suppose, that he went to the same hypothetical university John went to. Has *he* been to Vegas? And what did he think of it? Did he hate it? Was he indifferent? Or did he carry the memory of it like a guilty, joyful secret all those years?

In those moments between sleep and awakening they both rise inside me. Their voices speak, but only to me. They won't talk to each other. I beg them to be quiet. But now they are loose. Like a virus, they reproduce. They are caught in each other's moment, in an endless digital loop, spreading from one computer to another, from one mind to another, overtly conducting a youtube war.

But I didn't ask for this. I turned off the television. I subscribe to no papers. I listen to music stations on the radio and turn the volume down when the news comes on. In that I am like most people. I suspect Abu Karim did not care for the news until he found that he was part of them. And John, I think, is just a regular guy, with a sweetheart back home and a mother who writes him letters every week, and hopes he drinks plenty of water in the heat. Go to them, I say. Go to your mother, your sweetheart, your high-school coach, your small-town haven. And you, Abu Karim. Go to your heaven, if you are a believer. And if not, go to the place where us atheists go, into a nowhere that is everywhere, where our atoms, our quantum, live as long as the universe itself will exist. But go. I shall erase every last copy of you. I shall destroy the software that is able to decode you. I will eradicate all knowledge of the video format that holds you. Go. Go back to your war, and leave me to mine. I do not want your ghosts.

Eliot once said that he had seen birth and death, but had thought them different. The magi return to their kingdoms, but they are no longer at ease there. Frost said that home is where, when you have to go there, they have to let you in. Where will John and Abu Karim go? Can they return to their places, to the old dispensation? And if they did, who would let them in?

"Do it?"

"Confirmed."

"Ten seconds to impact."

Explosion. Black smoke. A voice says, "Dude," and nothing more.

Were they brought together, across half a world, for birth, or death?

Recently I visited the Kruger Park, a place far removed, at first glance, from the world of explosives, improvised or otherwise. I saw elephants and cheetahs, antelopes and rhinos, but the animals I liked the most were small. Black, ungraceful, the dung-beetles congregated wherever there was fresh dung. They burrowed inside it. Their arms gripped the fresh, moist, earthy shit and molded it. Diligently they formed it into balls, some much larger than themselves. Diligently they rolled the balls across the tarmac and into the bushveld beyond.

The dung beetles lay their eggs inside the balls of dung. Their young eat through the compressed excrement and, as they reach the outside at last, they open wings and fly.

A STAIN ON THE STONE

Nick Mamatas

I'm not going to bother with the slow build here, or the twist ending. So here it is, right up front: back in the summer of '84, Ricky Kasso lured Gary Lauwers out to the Aztakea Woods and spent the night torturing him in a drug-induced haze before killing him. You know the story already too; Kasso was the "Acid King" and deep into heavy metal and *The Satanic Bible* . . . as heavy as a seventeen year-old kid gets about anything. Kasso wasn't very smart; he was just another overprivileged twat from Northport Long Island. And Ricky, mostly as a joke only he found funny, demanded that Gary say, "I love Satan!" while he stabbed him. Gary shouted back, "I love my mother!" and then died. Two of Ricky's friends, Jimmy Troiano and Albert Quinones, were there, but they were all so cracked out of their minds that they probably didn't even realize how many times Gary has been stabbed, or that Gary's eyes weren't working anymore after being gouged with a stick. Albert even dragged Gary back to the scene twice when Gary, a pretty big kid, broke free and tried to run.

The scene was a large boulder, left by the retreat of the

glaciers that made Long Island the peculiar cigar-shaped stretch of sand it is. That boulder is where Northport High School's Knights of the Black Circle had their meetings. That's where Gary died. That's where Ricky had painted a message that proved just how ridiculous this whole wretched scene was:

SATIN LIVES!

Long Island in the 80s was all about the metal. Yes, there was WLIR, which played the The Smiths and The Cure for the shivering knots of gay nerds who hid in the art room during lunch, and there were even pockets of hip-hop. Strong Island represent and all that! But metal ruled. The high school talent shows were one pimply-faced guitarist after another, counting to themselves and tapping their foot while murdering Dokken on their mall-bought flying-V axes. But it wasn't the metal so much as it was the religion that was the problem. There was a girl in my school named Felicia, who was pretty with dark curls and nice rack for a petite chick, but she was a bit of a weirdo and her mother was worse. Felicia's mom wore a muumuu everywhere and weighed three hundred pounds. Once, at the King Kullen, she'd bought some plastic wrap and rubber gloves and mayonnaise and the total was exactly $6.66. As far as the kids in Drama Class (all dirtbags, not queers, as it counted as an English credit and didn't involve much reading) were concerned, that was proof positive. Personally, I was much more interested in what bizarre sex thing she might be doing with plastic wrap and rubber gloves and mayonnaise, but then I always had a taste for the odd. For everyone else, *six-six-six!* was all they needed to hear. Felicia was exiled to the nerdy fringe of the social circle, except insofar as she gave head on the first date, which she did. A lot.

I needed a job to pay for my car, but I wasn't going to mow lawns for sons of bitches for five bucks an hour or shelve stock at the King Kullen, so here was my idea: I'd give kids the occult tour of the North Shore. Where they tried the witches in Port Jefferson back in the 1650s. Yeah, it never made the history books in the way Salem, Mass did, but because the local colony only fined people for witchcraft. Amityville, natch. Kings Park Psychiatric Center, which was mostly closed and had plenty of dead buildings to poke around in. I'd even found the tracks to the old rail spur that led right into the hospital and made up some story about crazies being chained to a pump trolley and forced to travel along the spur all night as punishment for fighting or masturbating. The apex of the tour was the Lauwers murder scene, and the big rock. I'd break out a Thermos full of Jagermeister, a few hits of acid—or whatever I could buy that could be passed off as acid—and I'd collect twenty-five bucks a head. Then we'd all go to the diner and eat disco fries till sunup.

SATIN LIVES! became the bane of my fucking existence. I spent a lot of time reading up on Kasso. I knew he was the son of a football coach, a fact which always got a few hoots and guffaws from the crowd I'd lead into Aztakea. That two months before the murder he'd been arrested for disturbing a grave and that Gary Lauwers had been with him. Ricky and Gary were friends of a sort, but the only things they had in common were drugs and their Halloween fright mask version of Satanism. After Gary swiped ten baggies of angel dust from

Kasso, Kasso beat him up, but not too badly. The next meeting of the Knights of the Black Circle was going to be a set-up to teach Lauwers a lesson, but Ricky just went a bit too crazy from drugs and psychosis, and the other two dipshits didn't do anything to stop Kasso.

That's not the story I'd tell. I'd explain that Kasso had dug up a human skull along with Lauwers and ever since that night, things had changed between them. Kasso was wild-eyed from acid; they called him "The Acid King" at Northport and once, at a party, a girl he was making out with had a bad trip just from all the LSD in Ricky's saliva. He'd play Priest and Ozzy backwards constantly to get messages from his dark lords. I'd copied some of the LPs onto cassette and would play them backwards as we walked through the woods, flashlights casting the tree limbs like bones. When it was just us guys on the tour, we'd inevitably play a bit of *Star Wars* in the fog; with girls around, everyone was a bit cooler and darker. Some of the girls even prayed, or at least said, "Oh Jesus, Oh Jesus!" almost in time with the warped tunes from my box. The swallowed syllables of the music and my little patter would really make the girls shiver and want some manly protection.

I'd explain that a black crow came to Ricky—one time I even lucked out and a bird started cawing in the distance—and the crow demanded blood. So Ricky decided to bring Gary Lauwers out to the woods, the woods where Satan would talk to Ricky in the form of a tree and tell him black secrets of the occult. Someone would crunch through a pile of leaves noisily, and I'd gasp and shine my light on their feet.

"There," I said, every Saturday night. "There's where the body was. Where Ricky would bring kids to see after bragging about his murder at school. It took two weeks before anyone told the cops. It wasn't just Ricky who was in the grip of Satan, it was all of them. This is a sick society; we like to watch a kid die and rot, be all smelly and bloated, staring up at us with red gouges where his eyes used to be. Eye sockets squirming with little white maggots, a silent jury of our sins." Then the light would go under my chin. "Don't think you're any different, any of you. You're here now, aren't you? Looking for a little dark magic? Hoping to find something out here? Well, don't worry, you want the face of evil, just look in the mirror." A bit of silence for effect, then I'd say, "Come on."

I'd stop at a few different places, like the stations of the cross gone Widdershins. "Here's how far Gary got the first time he ran, but Ricky caught him and tackled him. Ricky was still the football coach's kid, a strong kid, a fast kid. He dragged him back to where the party was. This way." We'd walk some more. "Here was the tree Jimmy Troiano was leaning against the whole time, dusted out of his fucking mind. He thought he was watching a cartoon." Troiano's face was full of scars. He'd do anything to make friends, including trying to hang from a swing set by putting the swing-hook in his mouth. Jimmy Troiano had teeth like fangs. I'd shine the light and there would be a black-and-white pic of Troiano, blown up and glossy, right where I'd tacked it.

Then, closer, to a little clearing. "Here's where Ricky stabbed Gary a dozen times, and started screaming—" and I'd do a harsh stage whisper, "say you love Satan! Say you love Satan you little fucking bitch! Satan is your lord and master!" and Gary wouldn't scream, he wouldn't give in. He'd just wail, "I love my mother, I love my mother . . . " I'd wail that lightly, like I was playing Oliver in the school play, which I did as a freshman.

The big boulder was right behind me at this point in the tour. I knew the area like the back of my hand from my own poking around. The rock had a lot of moss on it near the bottom, and was under a thick canopy of leaves, so it was hard to see in the dark. "And then Ricky gouged out Gary's eyes. He told him he was doing it because he loved him and he didn't want him to see the torments of hell. 'I love you more than your whore mother, Gary, you dirty motherfucker.' " I made that part up.

"Say you love Satan!" I'd say again. Chanting. "Say you love Satan! You're going to die, but Satan lives! You die, Satan lives! You die, Satan lives!" Then I'd swing my big cop maglite to illuminate the boulder and it would light up the night like the moon and the kids would jump right out of their skins. "SATAN LIVES!"

After a few seconds, and if everyone was sober enough, a girl (always a girl) would say. "That says 'Satin lives.' "

There'd be a few *huh?*s or some laughs, depending on how sharp the crowd was.

"Yeah, Ricky was too high to spell very well. The other guys were all drop-outs and stuff. Nobody noticed."

"Maybe they weren't Satanists. Maybe they were just gay."

"Yeah, and Gary gave Ricky a shitty blowjob," some guy would say.

"What are you doing, talking about getting a blowjob from

some guy," another person would say and then the tour would degenerate into dumb animosities and it would take me twenty minutes to get everyone back to my car. This is why I collected the money after Kings Park, but before Northport.

People liked the tour, and there was good word of mouth around the dirtbag set, and even the couple of black kids in the area expressed an interest in attending, but there was a downside too. I *became* "Satin," for one thing. That's a good nickname for a stripper or a pimp from the 60s, not for a long-hair from Long Island.

"Wanna go do something sometime," I'd ask a girl. "I got a car now."

"Sure, Satin," she'd say. "Should I bring my boyfriend for me, and my brother for you?"

Sometimes I'd walk down the hall between classes and kids would sing bow-chicka-bow-bow as background music for the movie of my life. I got a couple of people shoving anti-gay Chick tracts in my locker, plus the ones about *Dungeons & Dragons* and heavy metal, which were amusing at least. Then it started hurting the tour. I'd go through the whole two-hour spiel in Port Jeff and Kings Park, then over to Amityville before looping back around to Northport and get everyone up to the rock and then someone, and sometimes everyone, would scream, "SATIN LIVES!"

One time, four guys I didn't really know, from Wading River high school, broke out and started singing "YMCA," even doing the Y, M, C, and A-shaped arm moves as they danced around. Even I had to laugh at that one, but business really dried up after that.

The last time it was just me and Felicia. I almost cancelled the tour, but she said she'd pay double, to make it worth my while. I was tempted to tell her to think of it as a date and get a little head, but I try to be a good guy. It was weird though, with just one person. She wanted to sit in the back seat like I was a chauffeur, and she sipped the Thermos full of Jager all dainty, like it was lemonade from a crystal goblet or something. I had to say, "Everything okay back there?" a few times, because she was so quiet. I felt like her dad or something.

Anyway, we did Drowned Meadow, the little area in Port Jefferson where they tried the witches, and Felicia gave me this awkward smile and said, "I live right there." She pointed to a pre-development house across the road, with flaking paint on the porch and tiny windows. "My mother hates you guys. Let's just go to the next stop."

And we did. We snuck into King Park and I showed her the track, and then we slipped in through an open into the giant Building 93, which looked like it was abandoned in a hurry. Rusty bedframes left in the middle of hallways, medical files splayed open and kicked around, even suitcases spilling with old clothes and black-and-white photos from the days when men wore hats and nobody wore jeans.

Then it was the long trip to Amityville and the murder house. She decided to sit up front then, and asked to put the radio on the college station instead of WBAB, which is what everyone listened to because it played a lot of Zep and G&R. Weird ambient grinding noises, punctuated with flutes, came out of the tinny speakers. She said it was relaxing. The house was the usual shit part of the tour, but she stayed close to me the whole time and as headed to Aztakea she drank a little more and our knees touched as I drove.

I had the only flashlight, so Felicia stood close by me, often grabbing my arm when she felt the mud and leaves shift beneath her feet. She was wearing sandals and socks—like I said, weirdo—so she felt almost every little twig. I did my usual spiel, the here-and-there of it all, leading Felicia around in a spiral leading to the boulder.

So, what do you think? We come across Ricky, his neck red and cricked from his prison suicide, knife in hand and fire in his eyes? Or poor old Gary, gaunt and covered in burns, arms out and hands grasping as he stumbles around blindly? Maybe Felicia's mother, skyclad and all jelly-like planes of flesh, holding a cat on the rock and praying to the Earth Goddess? Or **SATIN LIVES!** gone and replaced with blasphemous letters from a tongue men were not meant to see, that drives us insane?

Hell, I'd like to tell you what happened was that I finished hissing "Satan lives! Satan lives!" and flashed the light to the boulder and showed her **SATIN LIVES!** and she freaked, then laughed, then looked a bit sad. Then Felicia stepped up to me, chest out and chin up like she wanted a kiss and I said, "So, yeah. Satin lives," and gave her one and she liked it, then I put my fist in her hair and she liked that too, and then she pressed against me and guided me to the boulder and undid my pants and gave me a mint sloppy BJ.

And that is almost all that happened, except that when Felicia gave me that sad look, she also started talking. "Wow. My cousin knew these guys, back in middle school. They were all really sweet, even Ricky. Especially Gary. Even when he was totally fucked up, he was nice about it. He'd steal shit, money from his parents, or from a store, but then spend it all on other people. He gave away hundred dollar bills at the roller rink once, and bought this kid a motorcycle with his dad's credit card. Even Ricky wasn't bad. They were just all so fucked up. Fucking suburbia fucks kids up. The first crime Ricky ever did was stealing from the church, can you imagine? It was a container of Hi-C fruit punch." Then she stepped up to me for her kiss, then with her little hands on my shoulders and chest led me to lay across the altar of the stone to better undo my fly and unzip me.

About halfway through, she started whimpering. Her tongue got cold. I said, "Hey, what's up, Lish?" and she looked up at me, her eyes wet in the foggy beam of my flashlight. "This is so fucked up."

"Yeah," I agreed.

"Look, you're a nice guy. I like you," Felicia said. I didn't even get to say "Thanks," before she said, "My father molests me. Every day since I was three." Then she started to cry silent tears, like she had to every night so she wouldn't get caught. Jager and dinner rose to my throat, and I vomited all over the stone.

MR. WOSSLYNNE

Michael Cisco

At the end of my street lives Mr. Wosslynne, that no one has ever seen. He is ensconced, I imagine, in his freezing house yet. You might want to imagine a cold candle when you try to summon up a picture in your mind, the better to understand me, or the better to enter into the spirit of my narration, if you're so inclined. Conjure a mental impression of a soft, palpable darkness, a little cindery, but limpid too. This doesn't work, it doesn't make sense, but try anyway. It is an indoor darkness, and not the brittle kind that shuts out the daylight, which can be broken by a single errant shaft of sun, but rather the captured night that gets caught flowing through houses like the clots of hair that stop up drains. Now, the candle: it should be a pale white, almost blue, like a tube of snow, and the flame is blonde and cool, completely still, shedding wanness into the air without illuminating anything.

If you can see that, then you can surely see Mr. Wosslynne, who is the inhabitant. The house must now be permitted to congeal out of transparency around the candle and the darkness; the house is all made of brick, with small-paned windows that swing out on curved metal arms, and the number 247 appears by the front door on three small tiles held by a little black iron frame. I haven't the energy at the moment to relate the reasons for my association with Mr. Wosslynne, who tenanted this house, but that there were reasons should not be overpassed in haste; it's only that, were I to present them, I would necessarily be required to dilate this account farther than any reader's patience would warrant, and, confronted with the unfortunate choice between boring the reader and mystifying, in this case I prefer to remain mysterious. It should be enough to say that we shared a certain rare interest, although I was the sheerest dilletante in comparison with Mr. Wosslynne, and that we found in each other an uncommon opportunity for upbuilding conversation.

He isn't invisible. It would not be true to say that he can't be seen, only that he isn't seen. No one can be found who is competent to describe his appearance, and it is probable that he has never appeared to anyone. One is aware of him, can carry on conversations with him, and I have, but only something like a gesture will register, if it is possible to imagine a gesture without a face or a hand to make it. To represent it to another, you have to say something like, and then there was a depreciatory gesture, or, then there was a noncommital opening, or, there was an eager attitude.

The owl at the end of the street used to hoot from Mr. Wosslynne's eaves—such an odd, muffled sound, like an ocarina in a cork-lined basement. Mr. Wosslynne always paused in whatever he might be "saying" at the moment when that owl called, with an introspective note in its call, or more like a private chuckle I thought, so it came to seem as though the owl were interjecting into our "conversation." The pauses didn't last long enough to frustrate me. Mr. Wosslynne never noticed anything of that kind; he was habitually either oblivious or indifferent, if those are distinct enough ideas to separate without pleonasm, to my sentiments and exhibited an invarying tranquility all his own when in my company. While he would appear to become nervous or slightly restless now and then, in time I realized that this was not so much an expression of feeling as his way of signalling to me that he would prefer then to be alone, as he usually was. This was Mr. Wosslynne's "tact."

Then I would shed the veils of Mr. Wosslynne's house in the space dividing his door from the pavement and draw the acronychal light into my lungs with a weary, disembodied feeling. As I would walk back to my own door, I would gradually draw fresh strength from the dishevilment a heavy rain or strong wind had left behind in the town, the branches in the street and the sagging front gates hanging half open, that I so love to see.

Gradually the enervation that was the normal after-effect of my conversations with Mr. Wosslynne would become lightness, and I often felt a bracing freedom of movement in my limbs. My own speech and expression seemed to me, as I inwardly observed them, to become a little exaggerated, as though I'd been drinking. There was in particular one sensation, very difficult to describe, that was similar to what I've experienced in my altitudes; my spirit would seem to spin inside me, my heavier and more inert body lagging after the motion, so that

I seemed to wear it like a ponderous armor. Yet the movement of my spirit was completely unrestricted; my body turned into a dense colossus with my spirit frisking inside it. I'd speak, and my voice was a blast that shook the walls; my inflections were grotesquely broad, my smallest gesture became a grand sweep. The more sensibly precarious my self-control became, the more my self-awareness was intensified.

I never worried about the impression I might make in this condition because I was usually alone. It was not so strange to be alone then; that section of the city, perhaps the city all throughout, was steadily dwindling. I suppose this kind of alteration is not remarkable in the history of very old cities, and that they wax and wane like glaciers. Certainly there was no question of emergency; I believed the people were simply and unhastily taking themselves away elsewhere. The crowds I used to see on the corners, especially toward the end of the day as the lamps were being lit, shrank to knots of two and three, and at night the noise of the city came from far away. A steady, tidal yawn. I could stop whatever I was doing, knife in midair, to listen for any length of time, without hearing any sound from nearby. It was always as if it were snowing heavily.

Mr. Wosslynne was expecting me, but I had to buy him some cigarettes first. Mr. Wosslynne smoked incessantly, at least in my presence. Somehow his house didn't smell at all of smoke, nor did I find I left his house with the smell of cigarette smoke in my clothes or in my hair, which in any case one generally doesn't notice until washing one's hair after an interview with *the smoker.* Nor did I see him smoke. A lit cigarette could however always be seen, invariably in its place, an appealing little dimple in the edge of a superb black ashtray with a cigar company's name in gold on the side. "PARNERGA." Perched on the cigarette's tip would be a slender, unperturbed plume of smoke drawing a straight line to the rafters. It's possible I might have seen a cigarette or two somewhere else, I seem to recall something like that, but not distinctly, and neither do I remember how I started bringing Mr. Wosslynne packs of cigarettes, but it was one of those things that I'd imagined couldn't be stopped once they've started.

The elevator buttons are like discs of snow that light dull peach-colored fires behind them when pushed. I enjoyed the suave glide of the doors and the smooth motion of the elevator. That's my mailbox in the lobby wall. I looked inside. No messages. Who delivered them? Who swept up? The city seemed virtually evacuated, but if anything I felt an increase in the indeterminate presence in the streets and buildings, as though invisible, silent immigrants had taken possession.

Outside a huge shoal of birds swooped past in the air by the railway trestle, arcing round forming two groups, to return to their tree, like it had all been a joke that didn't turn out. I decided there were more and more birds those days. A flurry of wind jostled me and nearly plucked my hat from my head. I reached up to steady it (jolted my glasses with the corner of my cuff) and then, when the air was calm again, I lowered my hands and looked at them. They looked old, the skin creased and seamed like elastic tissue paper. They should have gifts buried in them. Now and then my attention untethers and follows every thing that presents itself; I don't like these states, I feel under a spell. A burst of song erupted by my ear. One of the birds was standing on top of the brick wall, and I saw a gear under the wing as it lifted, and the being flew away. Walking to the corner I noticed a clicking sound—the bead on my hat's chin ribbon tapping against me with each step. Did it always click like that? I wondered. If it did, then I've been ignoring it effortlessly all this time, I thought.

Lately I had been having difficulty buying cigarettes, his kind of course but then any kind—all the stores were always closed, though lit just the same. After a startling consultation with my watch I ventured to try a door, and found it open. The store was empty, with no one even minding the counter. I supposed the he, or she, might be out of sight in the back of the store, the 'back' I supposed they had. It felt curious being in the store alone. All the same the register and the counter together seemed to trace a form, the way sometimes a chair will, especially one that has been worn characteristically, or the way sometimes a cast-off garment will actually always do. Also the aisles suggested forms, the roundness of the cans stacked on the selves suggested the size of hands to grasp them, same for the width of boxes, the dimensions of doors and windows, all conformable.

I leant over the counter and simply took one, then several, packets of Mr. Wosslynne's kind of cigarettes. I then placed an amount of money commensurate with what I calculated to be their price on the counter, noticing then that the till was ajar. I opened the drawer. It was empty—not even a penny. I looked to see if there really were no money, inexplicably still unsure that the drawer was empty even though I could plainly see that not a penny was there. I arranged my money quickly and firmly shut the till, and the compartments in the drawer measured my fingers.

This one-sided exchange took far longer than it should have done; I ran the distance to Mr. Wosslynne's house very quickly, and arrived without a trace of fatigue. I was anxious to be even a little late, perhaps because I had always previously been strictly punctual and so I had no idea what sort of response I might meet with; while the subject had never come up, I was enough in awe of Mr. Wosslynne to fear his disapproval. A disagreeable, coiling, ever-changing and weak sensation as it were throbbed in me while I strode up the path to his door, and at the same time my speedy running had left as its residue a whirling, startled and unsettled agitation in my mind. I nearly felt exalted.

My ring went unanswered, and, as my thoughts cleared, I fretted a bit at the thought that perhaps Mr. Wosslynne ignored me in disgust. I had never known him to go out, and for that matter he had never cancelled or postponed a meeting: we met, invariably, at the same time. Of course, I knew he did go out, but I understood without needing to be told that his comings and goings were not of the usual kind, making it pointless to try to include them in ordinary social calculations. There never could be any question of Mr. Wosslynne being there, as it was necessary to believe he was, but only whether he were receiving.

Time passed, and I decided to leave, first slipping the packet of cigarettes into the mail chute, listening for the slide and soft pat they made inside. There was a face in the window as I walked past the house, stopping me in my tracks because Mr. Wosslynne had never used his windows in that way, he would have had to "crouch" by the sill and peer out, "the glass fogging in front of his nose," so to speak, and I didn't have to see it clearly to know certainly it wasn't Mr. Wosslynne's face. There was simply no question of that, although, as I've never seen Mr. Wosslynne's face, I can't actually account for my being as sure as I was. I did have to look closely for a moment, over the brick wall, to see it was my face. It blinked, and swayed, as I did. But it shouldn't have been gazing out at me as I passed.

I went back around, through the gate, and to the side of the house. My face was still there in the window, blinking, mouth a little slack—my reflection as far as I could tell. It was livid pink and orange, the color seemed more intense than it should have been in the dim light just after sunset, and it hovered in a gap of darkness between the sill and the blind, which had been left a little raised.

Gradually, as I looked on in defiance of the idea that I was spying, my face drew closer, and my gaze went through the apertures of its eyesockets. (These were overhung by shadows that leaned down over the cheeks as I drew closer.) Beyond the window I could see a plain room with two beds in it, jutting out with their feet set against opposing walls and the heads, without bedsteads, separated by a narrow space about wide enough for a man to sidle through. There didn't seem to be anything else in the room. When I withdrew, there was no reflection in the window.

Later that evening another strange thing happened as I stood in my bathroom. I was examining my face in the mirror: there's a subtle asymmetry to my features that people find a little off-putting. I saw all the world's mirrors were teeth in nervous jaws that open wider and wider, with a writhing around the teeth there. There was a dim shuddering tongue, mirror streaming from the teeth and frothing down charred lips to drop from the jaw in thick clots. They fell from the jaws in trembling clouds that floated in a way that disturbed me. My mouth watered, and I felt ill for a moment. My breath I thought tasted sooty, and I incessantly held it, to feel it inflate my chest, throat, mouth, sinuses, and even my skull, or so I picture it to myself. To my mind's eye, my breath was black, and filled my hollow body like smoke. A flash of cold engulfed me, my body tingled and that instant went numb. Again I observed the vibrating mirror jaw and the gouts of reflection oozing from it like a lanced abcess, and my body was nothing more than an outline in the wind, I thought, or a shape of cold particles.

What was this mouth? I thought I heard myself, and that seemed to cause me slightly to condense; with an abrupt hope of delivering myself, I labored to create the sound of speech, which I was not able to hear distinctly. I simply was pushing out, by an overall convulsion, a continuous sound. Nothing could be seen as I did this, as if my eyes were clenched tightly shut with the effort of making the sound of speech, although I was not aware whether or not I were seeing in the usual sense. Gradually, heavy mantles of weight, it seemed, dropped onto me one by one. Even when I felt certain, in a dreamlike way, that the crisis, whatever its nature, was over, and that my body was solid once more, I remained motionless where I was. I was certain I had to be extremely cautious for a time; as though I wouldn't manage to retain myself if I made any but the slowest, smallest, most tentative motions of which I was capable.

While I had no definite reason to think so, nevertheless there was no doubt at all in my mind that my experience had been in some way brought on by what I had seen that day in the window of Mr. Wosslynne's house. This unjustifiable conviction preyed on my mind, as I was expected at Mr. Wosslynne's house the next day, and I was utterly at a loss as to whether or not to go. I had difficulty thinking at all, and sat like a statue on the corner of my bed, staring inattentively at my hands. They shook. Watching them move on their own, sway to one side or other, had the effect of making my fright abstract, as though it were a property only of my hands. The fear I felt was entirely like that; it didn't get into my core, though it drove in near. In the tips of my fingers, I detected a series of very particular sensations—were they fingers or were they something else? There was nothing out of the ordinary in their appearance or behavior, although as I say the sensations were strange, but I wondered if I had the right word or idea of them. I was mentally comparing them to my notions of anatomy.

I didn't persevere to any conclusions, I simply put my hands aside onto the counterpane with an emotion of irritation and distraction. For a time I thought about nothing, but despair poured into me from somewhere, I was sure from somewhere but my thinking was distempered and I was nearly in tears, although even that felt uncertain, suggesting I had the wrong idea again. My every other thought and word was "something," "someone," or "somewhere." The thought of the gear under the wing came back to me with startling force. For an instant I thought I felt the wing in my bed, under the counterpane. I saw the birds explode en masse from their perches in the tree, hurtle through space and then return a moment later, and my thoughts were like the birds, liable to explode in all directions but perhaps not so liable to return. What I felt there under my hand was something like an inveterate chain of reasoning proceeding with irresistible logic from one point to the next; it was like a little spine made of cubical structures of gas or cubes of light, or it was like a piece of fine-linked jewelry at once supple and sparkling metallic, beautiful, but alarming like a frenzied ant hill. I wanted to gaze at it without participating in its activity.

"This is probably very unusual," I thought, "and other people don't have experiences like this. I wonder if I'm a machine, or an extraterrestrial, or a ghost, who's forgetting that other people exist. That would make sense of things, wouldn't it?"

I went to my window; there came, I know not by what association, into my mind a kind of story, or outline for a type of story, its form suggesting itself to me prior to any particular content. It would end with an abrupt shift in perspective; one character has an unusual way of looking at things, perhaps even a very strange way, and then another busybody character supervenes at the end to change the first character's story—it almost never happens the other way around—to restore the familiar. It comes down to which of these worlds the reader imagines himself to belong to, even though the purpose seems to be only to drift awhile in another current, and then get snatched out again. The first character might think that in some unremarked way he'd changed, or were discovering a truer nature beneath his apparent one, and mentally become a machine let's say. I was specially struck by the possibility that the change could take place unnoticed, even by the person who underwent it. He wouldn't be able to say anything about his transformation; he could only begin with the idea that he'd transformed. Then it occurred to me that the idea could just as readily end a story, by which I mean he could bring any line of events to an end at once with that idea, saying to himself, "but then, I'm a machine." Or he might well say, "but then, I'm human," by which he would mean something entirely distinct from what is usually meant by "human." He would be referring to what was *really* human, insofar as he stopped taking for granted, possibly for the first time in his life, his own frightening, alien, unknown humanity. In that case, it is the idea of humanity that transforms, from what it seems to be, ordinarily, to what it is. That is why there would *have* to be two characters, I thought.

The stillness in my room was complete. By now I could hear only the faintest sound from the streets. I looked out at the city's silent teeming. Simply by waiting this additional moment, I permitted the decision to make itself.

I couldn't be certain, the door might not have looked the same, and nothing had looked the same. My room in the soft brilliance of early morning light—the moment I'd left it, it became a memory, and imaginary. Nothing in my surroundings was quite recognizable to me; it was as though nothing upon which my eyes fell had the power to do any better than resemble something familiar to me. I found Mr. Wosslynne's house virtually by luck alone; it was necessary for me to visualize the route I normally took in a long kinked line leading from my door to his, measured in blocks. The blocks were, I believed, of more or less uniform dimensions. Around me were homes and shops, and I thought, of course, they might well be the homes and shops I've come to know in my long residence here. What a meager effort would it take, finally, to recognize them, I thought; it would be like making a very minor adjustment to a camera out of focus. Yet it seemed even that small exertion was too much for me. While I felt wide awake and alert, even exaggeratedly alert, there seemed to be an all but palpable fog in my mind as well.

By the time I'd reached the door to Mr. Wosslynne's house I felt myself growing unnerved. Frankly, I felt trapped between the shining day, a simmering panic, and the sheerly indifferent front of Mr. Wosslynne's house. I can't recall now whether or not I rang the bell or otherwise saluted, but my nervousness was strengthening every moment for no reason I could detect, a sudden fear that I might go to pieces in the street took hold of me—although, as always, the streets seemed absolutely empty—and without thinking I turned the doorknob. It turned easily and the door sprang open in my hand, which, parting the door from its jam, disclosed cool shade inside that absorbed me of itself. With the barest atom of volition I was inside Mr. Wosslynne's house, feeling as though it were a whim of the atmosphere of the place that I should come in. My relief was immediate, and I shut the door behind me, groping for words and uncertain I could make myself understood despite my self-confusion. I raised my head to meet the gaze of the presence that strode forward to greet me, but that was an illusion and there was nothing to be seen. It occurred to me the house was no more, nor less, familiar than anything else I'd seen today. Here I was, though, entirely certain I'd just been approached by someone—only an outline or movement in the air. But it didn't strike me that Mr. Wosslynne had come to meet me; this I thought felt like a woman's presence.

The furnishing of the house did seem to draw the outlines of a woman, in the sense that they conformed to what I considered to be recognizeably feminine gestures, and a woman's size. Mr. Wosslynne, needless to say, lived alone. I reasoned this was an illusion, and part of the unsettled state things appeared to be in that day.

I called, and heard music. Moving into a large room, where I had sat many times before on chairs not unlike the ones I saw, the music grew stronger, and I suddenly caught sight of a human being, sitting on a chair, facing me. I was fascinated, I confess I stared, and the human being clearly saw me, with that relentless human music streaming over me, pauselessly, as incomprehensible to me as silence in its insistence and continuousness. Was Mr. Wosslynne there at all?

After what seemed to me, but might not have been, some time, I found the human being had vanished, and the music had gone (I don't say "stopped"). There really was no material difference between the strangeness of the house and the strangeness of the street, and Mr. Wosslynne, if he were there, did not join me, therefore I began to think about leaving. My body responded on its own to the thought. I was turned and caused to go by some fiat of the air or the gravity of the ground. I moved through the door as if I were being driven along by a powerful wind or an ocean current, and my feet did not seem to rest firmly on the ground. My body folded, and, in this strange posture, suddenly I was flying along the street. I was hurtling uncontrollably along city streets, swerving around corners, now fast, now slow, jostling a little from side to side in mid air.

JONQUILS BLOOM

Geoffrey H. Goodwin

I never learned the way. Marcie always led me blindfolded. She'd pick me up, strap my eyes while we were in my apartment and then we'd get in a car. Other nights—when we didn't play the game—she had a Datsun so we probably rode in that. I felt like we were riding in her Datsun but her car was new enough that it didn't make distinctive sounds or vibrations.

She'd drive a while, stop, then weave me along a path that muddy-grass-squished until she'd squeak a gate open. We'd descend seventeen big concrete-sounding steps. My feet were all I'd hear. Once, I thought I heard street noise but I wasn't sure. It could've been an echo from the cavern at the bottom of the steps.

That's where she would take the blindfold off.

Last night, I smelled her perfume and thought of orchids. She always smelled like different fresh petals. That's what I did for a living. I arranged bouquets for Gary's Floristry. It's peculiar how often I imagined her. Nonstop: in dreams, in the shower, opening bills, watering plants, but especially when she'd come, late at night, to my apartment.

I met her at this weird club that I'd go to whenever watching black and white movies on cable didn't feel right. I always went to work at sunrise so the displays in Gary's window would look nice when he opened the shop at eight.

Silly as it sounds, the place where Marcie found me was called *Sir Dance-A-Lot's.* It had strobes and blacklights and was loud with vacant and sticky revelers, but when I got lonely it was company. People called me *the flower guy.* They knew my job and I'd wear these baggy spring-print shirts.

To me, she looked more significant than a woman should. The sort of person people write show tunes about. I couldn't play myself in the musical because I can bounce around and dance but went bald in my mid-twenties and can't cook. I eat too many TV dinners, so I'm pudgier than I was when I flunked out of college.

Marcie had on tightly laced black boots and was practically topless. This little band of shiny silver cloth went around her chest, leaving her tummy bare. She was sexy enough to make me want to hide in the bathroom, overwhelmed by surging desires and things I wanted to do to her.

Her long black ringlets bloomed from under this red leather cowboy hat that would've looked desperate on anyone else.

Blondes have never struck me as real, like plants made of vinyl that smell nice but feel greasy to the touch once you get up close.

This cover version of Madonna's song called *Into the Groove* came on. The vocals were sung in a pent-up and frustrated style. The DJs played it most nights and I would twist my shoulders around and punch the air with my fists. People cheered me on because they knew I liked it. Sometimes drunk people would chant "Flower Guy! Flower Guy!" But not very often.

Too many songs today are creepy and hyper—and this one was too, with smashing cymbals and metallic clanks—but I learned to love it because I was a fan of the original version.

Like I started to say, I went to community college for three semesters, studied botany, and met people and had a few romantic experiences with them. But the night I met Marcie was different than those couple of times in college. This was genuine, like I crossed over into some other level of life. Subtly trying to sneak a peek in her direction, I saw her shimmering breasts and short skirt first, but then her teeth captured me. They didn't sparkle but were perfectly centered and the right size for her mouth.

The next song started. Some people strut at dance clubs, all shoulders, but I don't like bumping other dancers unless that one Madonna cover is playing. I was sweating, so I went over to where the music was quieter and the floor wasn't crowded. The perky miss followed. It seemed ordinary because I didn't think she was coming after me. Not to sound crass, but Marcie looked like the kind of girl someone wealthy would keep. I didn't think of it then, but one night—dreaming of how her teeth sparkled and listening to Debussy—I marveled at how well maintained her illusion was, how hard it must have been for Marcie to look like she did.

"I'm Miss Levitch, but you can call me Marcie. They call you *the flower guy*?" was what she said. The smoke and the noise didn't swallow the words from her soft throat. She seemed friendly enough that I felt nervous. Normal, but frightened.

I looked at the gray acoustic tiles in the ceiling before I said, "Yes, Marcie."

I'm from rural Vermont. I don't have family or close friends anywhere near Wisconsin. I've spent time learning to protect myself from strangers. Maybe because people think they see a meekness or timidity about me.

A tingle of excitement crept up my leg like a black widow spider. I stammered and must've looked foolish. She was so enticing that even if Marcie and my mood were out of the ordinary, the need to touch her came over me in choppy waves. I remember that my leg, I think it was the right one, started quivering. I thought I was going to pee.

I just stared at her.

"A hot chick says hello and you frown?" she said. I knew I was supposed to act experienced with hot chicks, but I didn't know how. I've always been lousy at doing new things when I haven't spent enough time thinking them through.

I cleared my throat a little. My hand extended itself and started petting her hair. She looked at me funny, but didn't move to stop me. My heart started thumping.

"How old are you?" was the only thing that came, so I asked it.

Her glossy lips didn't move and I thought I'd screwed up. Even still, a bulge created itself in my jeans. Finally her stunning face shook around and said, "Quite old enough," and thanked me like it was a compliment. It might sound wrong or horrible, but I was so aroused that I couldn't think straight. I was disconcerted but Marcie turned my feelings around.

"Listen, this place isn't right for us to get to know each other. Can we duck outside?"

That made me queasy, but Marcie was my height and used my elbow to slide me past people, through the door, and into the night. Maybe people in the club, or outside smoking in the parking lot, saw us, but I was too out of it to notice if there were any witnesses. I was shaky so Marcie brought me away from the parked cars to the back of the lot where a big oak grew.

"Hey, I'm not tackling you and dragging you into the woods here."

"Feel free. I'm hazy, but the shock is passing. Are you, I mean, *you are* the most attractive display of a woman . . . "

"Re-lax, Marcellinus, I *want* to talk to you. Breathe for a minute."

My scary feelings prickled. No one knows that name or any way to tie me to it. I go by Mark—not a great name either—but tolerable. My parents died canoeing when I was twenty and I changed every bit of paperwork. I'm not "Marcellinus" to anybody. I'm Jewish . . . my last name's Glickman. My mom was flaky, into astronomy, astrology and odd stuff. With everything going on in early 1969, she was keyed up about how the Mariner 6 and 7 spacecrafts passed close enough to Mars to get good pictures.

Keyed up enough to name me after a planet. My parents realized how stupid it was and no one called me Marcellinus once I turned nine. After I changed it legally, I didn't tell a soul.

"How can you know my name?" I wanted her to like me

because she was so pretty but something was wrong. She said some dude at the club used it, then saw how much her lie creeped me out.

"Okay, it's not what you want to hear."

I got so anxious that I threw up on the oak tree. It oozed and spattered along the bark. My baby blue Hawaiian shirt became less baby blue in a few spots. It was very embarrassing. More than anything, I remember how I really wanted to pee.

"Ah, Marcellinus, I could tell you so much—but I shouldn't."

I shivered when she said it again. My eyes must've told her how much she frightened me.

"Please, *Mark*," finally sort of dribbled out my lips. I can't explain it, but when she understood, something vital in her smile made her gorgeous again. She waved her hands around for a moment, as if smoothing wrinkles in the air, and my insides went calm. Maybe it was because her name had that gentle *marce* sound too. Maybe not.

"Gotcha. Mark. Sorry if that seemed strange."

"How do you . . . ?"

"I don't want to tell that part yet."

Suddenly enchanted, I didn't need an explanation. All I needed was for this seraph named Marcie to tell me what she wanted. I felt the urge to start petting her hair again, but she stopped me when I reached for her. Instead, she removed her cowboy hat. Her breasts jiggled while she did it. The points of her little fingers fished around inside and pulled out what looked like a "joint." Normally that would get to me, but the serenity I felt was like special permission, an excuse to break my rules. It seems like I'd be okay with smoking a plant, even if it was illegal, but I tried it once when I was young and freaked out badly. That and my parents did it all the time.

"Is that pot?"

"Barely. Mostly sage, corn silk, horehound and licorice but there are some other bits and pieces."

I didn't care. She motioned around to the other side of the tree. I marveled at how sweet it was that she didn't even crease an eyebrow at the horribly nasty smell of my puke. When she pulled car keys out of her hat and unlocked the door to the nearest car, I wondered if she had a hidden set of keys for every car in the lot. This was before the humongous "joint." Things made even less sense after.

It was kind of like if an egg could poach and fry and get hardboiled all at once. I totally lost my skin, but somehow I could still caress her hair. We were crowded on top of each other in the front seat of her hatchback. I just lifted up the band of silver cloth that covered her tiny, perfect breasts and revealed moons more striking than Phobos or Ganymede. Then we were naked and at this contagiously cheap hotel that I'd never even slowed down near before. The "magic fingers" vibrating massage was going nuts all over the layers of skin that I also seemed to have lost. I felt like every inch of my body was being turned into a giant pickle.

I rolled around on top of her, kissing her lips and mouth. The only reason I know where I was is that we hadn't pulled the curtains.

Facing out to the highway like we were, I could see the neon green "Em rald Jung otor Inn" flashing for a moment while I took quick breaths. It was bizarre to be in bed with someone I'd just met—not even knowing where she came from, but feeling like she was all I'd been missing, like this was my lucky day.

I was on a roller coaster and even when my body slid to a stop, my mind whirled around for a few more loopdeeloops.

I woke up in my own bed, by myself, and it was three days later. I still had to go to the bathroom, even though I'd soiled the sheets. Friday night's mindbender had gone straight through to early Monday afternoon. I knew by the three papers outside my apartment door. I wasn't sore and nothing hurt too much, but my memory was completely fouled up. I started to feel uneasy. Gary, from the flower shop, had called to see if I was okay so I returned his message and told him I was sick. I started to tell him I was sorry for not calling sooner, but he was just glad to know that I was okay. And then it hit.

Marcie! Without her, I couldn't matter. Something like a pretzel of flab started to knot itself in my stomach. I started choking on my breath and almost passed out before I found her note push-pinned to my kitchen corkboard:

Dearest Mark,

Everything is okay. Everything *that you think happened actually did happen. And it was great! I just had to do some things, but I'll pick you up around this Friday's midnight. I know that some of this seems complicated or phony, but please trust in me for now. Explanations are forthcoming and all that . . .*

Everything,

Marcie

The note was short, which bothered me. My thoughts were more cluttered than usual. I kept trying to dredge up a slightly better sense of whatever had happened, but I only managed to get three conclusions: Marcie *was* real even though I didn't deserve her, something *was* so rotten in Devil's Lake State Park that I wanted to cry, and that Friday *was* soon enough that I'd survive, but I'd better put my act in order.

This is where my feelings began to get weird-boiled. I went to the bathroom to clean my pee off myself and I was thinking about how much I wanted to be with her again. When I took off my jeans, there was muck all over me—down where Marcie's mouth and face had been. I didn't think about it much. Instead, I thought how Marcie didn't look like she had been wearing that much makeup, but she had spent a lot of time down there. I was too caught up in waiting for Friday night. It washed off with water and looked like makeup as it went down the drain.

Friday did come, but the connecting days were torture. I'd wake up from the heart of sleep and reel my head around looking for her. I went to *Sir Dance-a-Lots* all four nights and sipped white wine. On Monday, the first night, I worried about having called in sick and getting caught at the club, but as the week progressed, I stopped calling and stopped caring.

Marcie had made it clear that she wouldn't be phoning me—just showing up when she said she would, so somewhere along the way, my phone and answering machine got smashed into scraps of plastic and metal. I ground my upper teeth into my bottom ones for like a hundred hours straight, especially when I tried to sleep.

My only relief came from remembering her moons, her mouth's inner curves, and the sculpture-perfect twinkle of her tiny teeth.

And then she reappeared. The buzz on my intercom jolted me from days of outlandish dreaming. Like a geranium that comes back in the early fall for no reason, there she was, standing radiant in my doorway. The joy, five minutes after midnight, melted me to tears. My apartment, my fingernails, and my baby blue Hawaiian shirt were all as clean as could be. I'd even spent time styling what was left of my hair. I hadn't done that in years. Instead of a bad comb-over, I had a rather slick one. Looking down, there were even loafers on my feet.

"Mark, it's so good to see you. What shall we do?"

"Everything," was my winded answer. We sat down on my beat-up corduroy couch. Being without her had drained me. I felt like I should curl up next to her and sleep, but I couldn't dare. I was too afraid she'd vanish.

I know that not very many people have been through something like this and I know that it's hard to talk about being sexually attracted to someone who is extremely beautiful without sounding like a pervert. Then again, I didn't feel particularly worthy of being chosen either. Marcie *was* fabulous. It's just that *fabulous* is a word with multiple meanings . . .

We did it again. This time on top of her car, sliding around on the hood while we made out like crazycakes, at a scenic stop by the side of Route 32. It was late and moonlit and I called her name loud, even though it was so different than anything I'd ever done. Marcie had plugged me in to a more fragrant, sensuous world.

It kept going that way. The nights without her seemed to get a little better. I took to sleeping in my closet so I wouldn't pace around. I felt safe, lying there in the dark for the days when she was away. When she pressed my buzzer, I'd be waiting and ready. I stopped eating, only craving the sweetness of her skin. I knew I was going downhill. The inside of my head got shot up with confusion and I didn't look quite as good as I used to try to look, but it was easy to accept. My hair boinked cockeyed and my face became grizzled . . . but, Marcie, she was Marcie—and that was clarity enough to keep everything else in place. I just wondered when I'd get to lift her skirt or pull down her jeans. I wanted nothing more than to return the mouth favors she'd been bestowing.

She was visiting more often. Concerns that she was seeing other people slipped away. I guess I got caught up in it all. She'd giggle and run her fingernails through my thatches of hair. The midnight movie theater for a showing of *Marnie.* In the rose garden of a mansion on Kindred Boulevard. The weeks spread out, as we got so close, more and more intimate, over twenty-six days.

Every bit of her was like a fantastic creature. I kept on sleeping in my closet. There wasn't any special reason for it, just less room for me to roll around waiting to get distracted. You can't imagine how much I wanted to uncover her sex and actually make love to her, instead of just receiving mouth favors.

Looking back, I didn't feel like the stallion that you'd think I would've felt like. A little part of me knew it was all overmuch. My arms and back would get sore from lifting and pushing my member into her. I started to call the intimacy of her mouth my "peapod" and she didn't mind. I had never, ever been loved by anyone like her. Not one bit. Her tongue was the most angelic thing in the world, like an eclipse.

Now, here I was a lucky man, but my back molars felt like they were getting shorter from my grinding. And I found strange raw spots of skin from jamming my softness against the friction of her tongue and teeth, too.

Anyway, I ignored any concerns because it felt like Marcie and I were destined to be together. Marcie was meticulous with the scheduling of her arrivals. I never knew if she was employed. Curled up on my couch one day, I asked if she had a job and she said, "The idea strikes me as interesting."

A few times like that, I felt like I should keep my lips from moving. I should just peck her on the cheek and act however she wanted me to act. It wasn't that I didn't want to know. It was that I didn't want to scare her off.

So, there, I've told it as good as I could remember, up to the last night.

Like I said, Marcie came smelling of orchids, with perhaps a hint of gardenia. Barely dressed in a white gossamer robe, she gently wrapped the blindfold around my eyes and drove—leading me to our secret cavern. Stumbling down the smooth-flat steps in the darkness, Marcie whispered about tonight, "finally being special." All my blood drained down into my genitals. Her temptations made the pressure inside me seem unreal and it was uncanny how wound up I was.

Then Marcie untied my eyes. We were underground, in the sarcophagus room. That's where, some blindfolded nights, she'd lead me. I know it sounds unusual, but she said it was a place where we could be alone and do anything, anything at all, that our hearts desired.

I couldn't get my eyes to look up at her unblemished face. My gaze kept dropping to her thighs, where her robe parted just a bit. She could tell I was staring and seemed okay with it.

In a fluid gesture, her smile sparkling now, she grabbed her robe's fluffy white collar. The cloth fluttered as it dropped to the stone floor. The raven strands of her hair seemed to breathe or pulse, subtly, in the darkness.

Her eyes glowed a sudden green. A pale radiance exuded from her skin. A crazy profusion of heat flowed toward me, spraying from her. I smelled some earthy bouquet, crackling underneath her scent. Marcie began to make an animal hum. I was enraptured by her soft murmurs, a rush of saliva in my mouth as I stared at her sex. Its lips parted delicately.

I distinctly recall her mumbling an apology, though that could be my wits playing tricks. A vision of her, soft like smoke, began to unfold before me. Small shoots and vines began to unfold from between her legs. The green tentacles grew thicker, reaching out toward me. As in awe of her unfurling fronds as I was, I wet my pants like you wouldn't believe.

Vines continued to hiss out of her nether regions, thicker and thicker until they were like wisteria bark. As preposterous as it sounds, I remember marveling at how quickly she sprouted, like kudzu.

It seemed to last that way for hours, for days. I was terrified and hypnotized, transfixed by the wonder of nature that was before me, perhaps naively hoping that I could still make love to this dream-creature.

Her face fell off—well, the sheets of latex, robotics and makeup that had made her into my Marcie. The wig of her hair tumbled off. Leaf flaps, like oversized jonquils, bloomed from where her face had been.

The room erupted with flowers, fecund tendrils seething with her very essence. I crumpled, gasping barely breathing in the rich drowning green of it all. As a visual person, her unblemished face should've tipped me off. Our faces are so exposed; up close enough, no one's skin is as flawless and unblemished as Marcie's had always appeared to be.

And I figured out how she knew my original name, Marcellinus. When I was eight, way up high in a maple, when I was trying to climb as high as the stars, I carved my name into the bark. It's got to still be there, in Northfield, Vermont.

They found me lying in the cemetery, they said. Facedown and muddy by the stone door outside the tomb. They said the door was locked but I didn't believe them.

Marcie had pleasured me too much for it to be any different than I've laid it out. They said the door couldn't budge—but that's where they gave themselves away. They claimed the name Marcie Levitch was engraved in marble. They insisted the granite door to the sarcophagus was wedged shut by a thick arm of bougainvillea.

My experiences were not the sort that can be imagined. I am not the sort of man to hallucinate.

Bougainvillea could never climb that flight of stairs, thriving in the darkness, unfurling without a miraculously bright light. It can't grow like that in Wisconsin. The perverse irony of their falsehoods is that I'm under lock and key, and the liars are free.

I told them everything, true like I told you, but they won't let me out. And I've been placed in this small room with barred windows, a tiny bed, a wooden desk and a musty journal lying open to a blank page. I'm using the note she left after our first night together as a bookmark. And I miss her.

INVASIVE SPECIES

Carrie Laben

The starlings were hit hard when the Conrads' barn burned. A few of them died as the smoke and flames swept the evergreens where they roosted; the survivors lost their shelter and their cattle-feed buffet.

Some resorted to the scraggly locust trees by the well, but bare deciduous branches offered no protection from wind or rain or owls. Some resorted to perching on the chimney. They fell asleep and never woke up. Meanwhile, the number of lost kernels of corn to be found in the tall grass was dwindling.

So, as the sun grew more fearful of getting too far from the horizon, the starlings began to move.

The first people to notice were the Bucks, who'd bought the place a quarter-mile up the road and were running horses on it. They were so new that Daniel Buck hadn't yet quit bragging about what a deal he'd gotten on the place, but they weren't completely stupid.

Janice Buck, for instance, knew that something was wrong before her eyes adjusted from the brittle outdoor light to the barn's dusk. Horse manure and hay had smells that she knew, and even loved a little—but today the barn's odor was wrong, tinged with more ammonia than usual. And when she could make out Marco's stall, the pony seemed lumpy. Swollen.

She ran, trying to remember everything she'd ever read about the various manifestations of bloat. In the shadows, Marco's skin seemed to be rippling or crawling. The thought of overgrown worms or bot flies made her hesitate; but he was her horse, her responsibility, and she had to help him.

She was a few steps away when the starlings took off, and even then her mind couldn't quite shape what her eyes were seeing into something sensible. The sound and the rush of air gave her the sensation of being sucked into a giant fan. Then the birds streamed out the open door, blotting out the sun, and were gone.

Marco raised his head and snorted softly. She was having visions of him bleeding, pecked, eyes gouged out—but he was fine, only his oats had been pillaged. He nuzzled at her, a little indignant, mostly just hungry. But the barn still didn't smell right.

When she went back up to the house to tell her parents what had happened, she didn't notice the starling that slipped through the door behind her.

❖

There was a line in front of the feed store when Dan Buck got there—not a Wal-Mart at Christmas line, but a knot of men and women using their trucks as windbreaks, smoking and talking in low voices. A handful of starlings were perched on the telephone line overhead, and their continual whistling chatter kept everyone on edge. One of them had learned to imitate the woman who read the weather on Channel 7 somehow and seemed eager to show the ability off. People laughed nervously, called the bird a floozy who didn't know wintry mix from her own ass.

"Yeah, they're enough to drive you crazy," Rick Morris said. "I was trying to eat my breakfast and one of the little fuckers took a crap right in my cereal."

Another band of starlings circled in to join the first. Kim Lyman picked up a rock from the parking lot and chucked it at them. The starlings roused and settled again, noisier than before.

When the clerk finally showed up and unlocked the place, half a dozen of the starlings swooped low over their heads in the doorway. Rick threw his hands up to protect his head and knocked one down, and stood on its wing with one foot while he crushed its skull with the other. Dan would have looked away, but after the night he'd spent he was no longer bothered by the sight of a broken bird. The rest of the starlings got through and perched on the tops of the shelves.

❖

By the time Joe arrived for the afternoon shift, Gladys had sold out of naphthalene, air-gun ammo, bird netting, glue traps and poisoned bait. Meanwhile, more starlings were getting into the building every time someone opened the door. The customers seemingly couldn't resist trying to knock them down; this was having more effect on the merchandise than on the birds.

On her way home she looked over at the Conrads' and saw that Angela's car was in the driveway. Without thinking, she pulled in behind it, and then she had to get out and knock on the door, because it would look pretty weird if she just pulled out again.

She'd grown up just over the hill, driven by here almost every day of her adult life. Seeing the charcoal crater where the barn had been, with the skeletons of the pines on one side and the silo listing on the other, was like a punch in the sternum.

Angela was in the kitchen, washing dishes. To her surprise Erik was there too.

"Shouldn't you be in the hospital?" she asked him. He was pretty bandaged up, especially around the hands, and his face looked brutal. No eyebrows anymore; skin pink and peeling.

"The hospital gets a lot less eager to keep your company when they find out you don't have insurance," he said with a chuckle. His voice was changed, too. "Besides, fire can't kill me."

"You sound awful sure of yourself."

"I'd have to be, to go running into the flames like a damned fool for a bunch of old books, wouldn't I?"

Angela, scrubbing hard at a pot, rolled her eyes.

"A guy who was born to be drowned can't be hanged. And he can't be burned, either."

The starlings perched on the top of the corner cupboard shifted with a dry sound of feathers on feathers. Gladys, always uneasy when Erik went on one of his prophetic rambles, turned to Angela and tried to change the subject. "So you've got the starlings, too."

"Of course. What can you do?"

"Going by what we sold today, people are trying everything short of tactical nukes to get rid of them."

"And it ain't working, is it?" Erik said from behind her.

"It's early to tell yet."

"It won't work."

He had that quaver in his voice that he got when he spoke shit that was going to come true; she had to shut him up.

"What are you doing to deal with them?"

"Putting up with them." As though to underscore Angela's point, a starling swooped across the room and landed a dropping in the dishwater. "We've been putting up with this sort of crap all our lives. I don't think Erik even remembers when the barn was built."

"Of course I do!" He coughed.

"No, you don't. I was four when the windstorm took out the grove, right? So you were one. And it took a year to get the lumber milled, with everyone in town being so prissy about touching it, and a year to get the barn up. So I was six, and you were three."

"I remember a lot of things that folks don't think I should be able to."

"It seems to me," Gladys said, interrupting, "that there's a lot more starlings involved than ever could have been on your place to begin with. They're in every house and barn for twenty miles around."

"It's airborne," Erik said, and she couldn't pretend she hadn't heard. "Contagious. Spreads by spores."

"So what about that silo?" she said desperately.

"It'll have to come down," Angela said, pulling the plug on the sink. "It's still burning inside."

"Hell."

"Yeah. Do you have any idea how much they charge for that kind of thing? To hire someone who'll make sure that it won't hit the house . . . " Angela shook her head, tossed the dishtowel on the counter.

"Why'd they do it?" Erik said, lurching up to look out the window to where the barn had been—no more prophecy voice, just the sad voice of the boy she'd once kissed at a school dance. "Fuck. We had it contained, if they would have left it alone."

"It couldn't last forever," Angela said. "Wood rots."

"Still. We had decades yet to figure something out, if the fuckers hadn't burned it."

"It was arson, then?" Gladys asked, fascinated and appalled.

"The police don't say so," Angela said.

"The police don't know shit." Erik settled back into his chair in obvious pain.

❖

The temperature dropped sharply during the night. Barnyard mud scabbed over with ice. Tomatoes and parsley plants and jewelweeds and asters died in silence.

Some of the starlings who hadn't found shelter died too. But only a handful.

When the sun rose, they were hungry again. Even in a house with central heating, night meant a lot of calories burnt. Another handful of starlings got too close to humans, cats, lit stoves, the fumes of Teflon pans cooking bacon. But only a handful.

Martin Dane left his mom and brothers in the kitchen, trying to get their spoons from their bowls to their mouths fast enough to avoid the darting beaks, and hiked into the woods for peace. Out at the tree stand he could see his breath, but the only birds around were some blue jays being angry at something far away.

He hadn't been there long when the leaves crunched below and Jake Marshall appeared with a cup of coffee and a paper sack sagging with burgers.

"Got a healthy breakfast there," Martin said, as Jake bit into a sandwich oozing safety-orange cheese.

Jake swallowed. "Might as well enjoy them while I can. Mae Norris says that if she can't get the birds cleared out of the building in another day or two, she's going to have to shut down before the Health Department fines her up the ass and the main office yanks her franchise."

"Didn't she get an exterminator?"

"She did, first day, but they won't touch the poison. And when the dude tried to fumigate, they just cleared out and then came back as soon as it was safe." He opened the bag again. "You want one?"

Martin nodded, and they ate in silence for a while. The sun began to take the frost off the world; a nuthatch landed on a nearby branch and they both startled at the sound of wings before they saw what it was.

"Last night, those fuckers actually managed to chase Badger away from his food dish and ate all the kibble," Jake said. "You know Badger and food. I think he hated it worse than when I had him neutered."

"He let a bunch of little birds like that keep him out of the food dish?"

"Every time he tried to get a bite they pecked his snout. Gave him a nosebleed, and now he's afraid of them."

Martin snorted.

"Yeah, well, regardless, I'm not going to let him starve to death. I finally got them all cleared out of the bathroom and fed him in there with the door closed. Took me an hour to clear one goddamn room." He sipped his coffee. "We gotta figure something out. It can't go on like this very long."

"My grandma says that all this shit is punishment on us for burning the Conrads' barn down."

"Your grandma's a nutcase. With all due respect, dude."

"Yeah, but . . . "

"First of all, everyone at the firehouse agrees, it was an electrical fire. The cops say so, too. Second, I distinctly remember your grandma saying that the fire was punishment on them for all that weird shit Erik does, so which is it?"

"I guess it could be both."

The shriek of a thousand voices rose suddenly from the direction of the road. Jake and Martin abandoned the remaining food and climbed out of the tree so fast that they might almost have jumped.

By the time they reached the nearest field, it had grown louder. Over the line of the trees, a great black mass pulsed like a heart, rippled, spread so that they could see the sky beyond, reconcentrated. Then the flock made a strange, almost percussive sound and streamed away to the east.

"That was over the Conrad's place," Martin said. Jake nodded. They ran for home.

❖

Gladys looked out the Conrad's kitchen window. "That's Jake Marshall's truck pulling in," she told Angela. "He's got Martin with him."

"Sure, everybody shows up now." Angela said, not looking up from Erik's body. "Vultures."

"Be fair. Jake's a good kid. He was at the fire."

"I know, I know. I'm just . . . "

Gladys nodded, and when Martin and Jake reached the door she sent them to tell Joe that she'd be late for her shift.

"It's Aunt Mary's fault," Angela said as soon as they were gone. "She's a registered nurse, you'd think she'd have some goddamn sense."

"What do you mean?"

"She came over to help change Erik's bandages, and she went and told him that people with bad burns can die from fluid in their lungs."

Every few seconds a starling would flutter in from the top of the bookshelf or the back of a nearby chair and try to land on his face, and Angela would flail at it angrily, and it would fly away again.

"I saw on the news last night that they're having trouble with starlings all the way in Depew now. Do you think it's getting worse?"

"Erik thought it was. I mean, it makes sense, doesn't it? When it was in the wood, it could only move so fast. But now it's airborne . . . "

"I heard Daniel Buck is talking about hiring one of those guys with a falcon to go at them."

"You think you can talk to him?"

"I'd better, I guess."

SHE HEARS MUSIC UP ABOVE

F. Brett Cox

At Exit 10 Olivia asks Peter how they're doing on gas. He checks the gauge and says they'd probably better stop. She asks not because she has any real sense of how long it's been since they last filled the tank but because she wants him to stop talking. He had begun to outline a theory of the fundamental differences between living on the coast, where they are both from, and living in the mountains, where they are now, and suddenly, with a certainty that startles her, Olivia realizes that, at the moment, she just does not want to hear any theories.

They take the exit and stop at the first convenience store. Peter suggests that they drive into the town whose name was at the top of the exit sign and is, according to the smaller sign by the convenience store, only a quarter-mile down the road. Olivia nods and looks out the car window, vaguely dissatisfied that he's still talking.

As they drive by the village common they see a group of people with musical instruments gathering on a small stage with a shell over it, and others arranging themselves in front of the stage on collapsible lawn chairs and blankets and on the lawn itself. Peter asks if they should stop, and Olivia says sure. He pulls over and parks. Olivia gets out of the car and immediately hears music. Not from the bandstand where the musicians are still gathering, and not from the radio in the car, and not even inside her own head. A woman's voice, a steady pulling melody as if a magnet had started singing. Not in her head but somewhere up above.

Life since college has been a mixed bag for Peter. He failed to parlay his undergraduate degree in computer science into one of the cyber-fortunes that at one time seemed to hang like ripe clusters of virtual fruit, ready for the picking; the fact that his was not the only such disappointment was little comfort. A return to school and a Master of Liberal Studies was intellectually fulfilling but unprofitable. A semi-random but wholly desperate application to a small university on the Massachusetts shore yielded a job in the registrar's office, where, to his surprise, he has not only remained, but advanced. His position as Registrar is relatively safe from economic fluctuations—students may enroll in greater or lesser numbers, but someone has to be there to register them—and he is good at it, keeping both faculty and administration content with his ability to arrange times and locations that flow smoothly and steadily through the academic day. A month after he started he met Olivia, two doors down in Human Resources. They have been together ever since. His parents like her; her parents are dead. Recently he has considered returning to his roots and enrolling in the college's online graduate program in Information Assurance, which he can do while continuing full-time in this safe and steady job with a retirement fund in which, three years hence, he will be fully vested. He and Olivia can afford to take weekend excursions such as their present trip into the mountains of central Vermont.

But next year he will turn forty, and while he has no reasonable grounds for complaint, while he understands completely that his best years lie ahead of him, he sometimes wonders what those years could possibly contain that would be at all different from right now. It is a perilous sequence of thoughts: things are fine now, but things could always be better, but how likely is that, and would it be a bad thing if they weren't, and are things indeed fine? Are they really? Olivia loves him, he is certain, but they don't talk like they used to. She is unfailingly pleasant and frequently passionate, and when he asks her how she is, her answers are always positive. Yet there are times when the pleasantries seem reflexive, the passion rehearsed, the answers slow in coming and brief when they arrive. There are nights when he cannot sleep and his present and his future churn within him like small sharks circling dead and bloody meat.

He looks at Olivia as they sit on a wood-and-iron bench to the left of the bandstand, behind the bulk of the crowd but still close to the stage. Her face is ever so slightly heavier than it used to be; he is as struck by her pale, unfreckled skin and the red silk of her hair as he was when they first met. Once, early in their relationship, he called her his Celtic beauty, but she gave him a dubious look and he never called her that again.

As the band begins to tune up he resumes the conversation they had been having before they turned off the interstate. He repeats that coastal areas, by definition, offer easy access; people can drift in and out at will and with little notice. It's easy to enter and easy to exit. If you're in the mountains, though, you have to make an effort to get there, and you have to make an effort to leave. Thus the shifting demographics of their college town by the sea, as opposed to the constants of northern New England: Yankees firmly planted for centuries; ex-hippies not far removed from their ex-communes; people who came for a skiing vacation and never left. Olivia tells him that the coast is home to plenty of old things and looks intently at a row of houses on the other side of the common.

Olivia's father died when she was in high school, killed in a collision not five miles from their tidewater Virginia home. It was the other driver's fault. Her mother held up brilliantly during the funeral and throughout the five years that followed before the tumor in her left breast metastasized. Olivia's father's death taught her that terrible things can happen for absolutely no reason, and her mother's final illness taught her that knowing the reason doesn't make any difference. Her parents loved her and she loved them with no significant complaints. Each loss was like a layer being peeled away from her, leaving raw and exposed the dizzy uncertainty of being alone in the world and the guilt she felt because she didn't miss them more than she did. When she met Peter she could feel a layer being added back on, slowly and carefully. It felt wonderful to begin with, and then it felt good, and lately it has not felt any particular way at all.

The band on the common begins their first song, which she does not exactly recognize—some old American standard or other. The sound of the band is white noise to the music that continues to hover above her, like the wash of the floor fan Peter runs to help him sleep at night but which never completely obliterates the sounds of the night: the furnace groaning on, a neighbor's dog barking, a car speeding away into the surrounding darkness. It does not occur to her to ask Peter if he hears this music; she knows she is the only one who can. The woman's voice draws Olivia's attention across the grass, wilted in the breezeless July heat, past the swing set on which a boy and a girl swoop past each other like scissors clicking open and shut, toward the middle house in the row of three that stand on the other side of the common.

Olivia knows she will cross the common and enter the house, but she does not want to just yet. She is thirsty. She looks behind her and sees a small strip shopping center, one unit of which is a grocery store. She tells Peter she is going to get something to drink and leaves him sitting on the bench.

The members of the band, like the members of the audience, are mostly older people, although there are a scattering of men and women Peter's age and younger. The musicians all wear green polo shirts and khaki pants. Each shirt has a left breast pocket bearing some kind of logo patch Peter doesn't recognize. The musicians are all wearing sunglasses, cheap knockoff mirrorshades that you can buy for a dollar at a roadside flea market. Their playing is surprisingly smooth, much better than Peter had expected, with only a hint of the dissonance of a group of musicians that has a limited amount of time to rehearse. The songs they play—"In the Good Old Summertime," "The Sidewalks of New York," "A Bicycle Built for Two"—could have come from a songbook a century old, and when Peter sees a page fall from the music stand of one of the trombone players, he thinks it looks yellowed, tattered. He is suddenly aware of the very old people sitting closest to the band, and the younger families sitting farther away, and the children running freely as their parents listen to the music, and he has the same feeling he has at night when he can't sleep and the sharks are circling. He tries to push it aside, assigns the twinge of wrongness he feels to other things: his mild dread of the tiresome drive back to Massachusetts, his continued indecision about returning to graduate school. The band is now playing "The Tennessee Waltz," and he thinks first of his grandparents dancing at his parents' twentieth anniversary party, and then of the story his mother had told him of his great-grandmother who died giving birth to her ninth child, and her second husband who died of an infected blister on his heel. He taps out the beat of the music on the arm of the bench; soon he is hitting the iron with the heel of his hand on the downbeat, *one* two three *one* two three, and he has to stop before he injures his hand. He does not understand his mounting anxiety; he has no explanation for why this tranquil place and this innocuous music, this idyllic summer day, fill his thoughts with the deaths of people he never knew. The late afternoon sun dips behind the maple tree that rises from the middle of the common. He feels a sudden chill and does not understand that either. He wonders what is taking Olivia so long.

The temperature in the grocery store is at least twenty degrees cooler than the temperature outside. When Olivia first arrived in Massachusetts from Virginia, many people asked how she could stand the southern heat, secure in their New England conviction that anything south of Maryland is the tropics. Rather than give them a geography lesson, she replied that yes, the South was hot, but everything was air conditioned—unlike New England, where air conditioning seemed largely confined to movie theaters and grocery stores.

The music above her is coming from speakers in the ceiling; the other voice she left on the common.

The glass doors of the refrigerated wall cases are fogged; she opens one, pulls out a plastic bottle of water. She doesn't recognize the brand, but there's a strawberry on the label. She is the only customer in the store. The woman at the cash register, who must weigh at least three hundred pounds, has enormous, dilated eyes; Olivia wonders if she's an addict on some kind of halfway house work release. Or do drugs make your pupils small? She used to know. There are many things she has forgotten and she would like to remember them. She pays for her bottle of water and walks out into the steady heat and diminishing afternoon light.

She crosses back to the common, where Peter sits on the bench, transfixed by the band. The music above her returns and grows stronger as she walks across the grass. Peter does not seem to notice her return. The boy on the swing is gone but his swing still moves; the girl's twig-thin legs stretch out from her thickly piled skirt as she pushes herself incrementally higher. Olivia walks past her, drinking the strawberry water. The boy's empty swing continues to rise. The music from the band recedes and the song above her grows stronger as she climbs the front steps of the middle house.

Peter is starting to panic. The other people on the common sit tranquilly listening to the band, but the dying notes of "The Tennessee Waltz" elicit images of a septic world where babies are fatal and blisters kill, and the crowd's polite applause conjures a vision of his own sterile deathbed. The afternoon light is starting to fade. The band director, who is notably younger than most of the rest of the musicians, takes off his sunglasses and wipes them on the hem of his shirt. He turns to the audience to announce the final song, and Peter is amazed at the size and darkness of his eyes, almost as if he still wore his sunglasses. The band director turns back to his musicians and raises his baton, and as the band launches into "The Stars and Stripes Forever" Peter looks across the common and sees someone on the steps of the middle house. A flash of white, a mist of red. Olivia? He looks again and this time clearly sees her open the door and enter the house. He rises from the bench and heads across the common; by the time he passes the empty, motionless swing set, he is running.

❖

The song is all around her now.

❖

The red brick Federal style house has undoubtedly been there longer than anything on the band's program. The symmetrical windows are bordered with green shutters; the yard is overgrown but not neglected. Steps set parallel to the front of the house lead up to a screened-in porch that wraps around the left front and side of the house. Peter leaps up the steps, but when he gets to the porch door he is not sure what to do. Knock? Call out? He tries the door; it pulls easily open and he steps in. The porch is empty: no plants, no furniture, nothing. The only entrance to the house itself is a white door with a brass knocker. There is a half-empty plastic bottle of water on the floor by the door. He knocks repeatedly, calls Olivia's name. No reply. He turns the brass doorknob and has to lean in with his shoulder and push before the door opens. He leaves the door open and walks inside.

The room he enters is like the yard, cluttered but not ignored. A sofa bracketed by lace-covered side tables, a recliner, a coffee table and scattered chairs date from no particular era, but the walls are done in a frantic Victorian wallpaper. Opposite the sofa above a bricked-over fireplace hangs an elaborately-framed painting of mountains dropping to a stormy beach; small boats dot the waves while ill-defined figures wait on the shore. There is no television and no phone, no books or photographs, but there is a girl of about ten or eleven sitting on the sofa, thin legs crossed at the ankles, hands folded serenely in her lap. Her dress is too thick for July, her hair is the same color as Olivia's, and her eyes are the same as the band leader's.

Before Peter can apologize for walking in unannounced and say he is looking for his friend who came in just a minute ago, the girl gets up and walks to the far wall of the room, where there is a white door with a heavy brass knob. She opens it and beckons him to follow her.

This room is lined with shelves filled with books, old, oversize volumes. Against the far wall is an enormous old roll top desk, closed and locked, with a padded wooden desk chair on wheels. In the center of the room stands an aquarium tank in which swims an enormous fish. A boy about the same age as the girl stands beside the tank. He wears a shirt and trousers that appear to be made from the same material as the girl's dress, and his eyes are closed.

Peter walks up to the tank. The fish appears to be some kind of eel. Its head is disproportionally large, its eyes protruding and black, its mouth filled with needle-thin fangs. Its body is covered in a cloud of fine, waving antennae. It circles methodically within the tank, adding a quick burst of speed each time it reaches the corner nearest the desk. It looks like a picture Peter had seen in a grade-school reference book of sea creatures from the aphotic depths, creatures so ominously unlike anything he had ever seen before that he had dreamed of them for a week afterward.

The girl walks over to the tank and removes the eel, which immediately falls limp in her hands. The boy reaches into the left pocket of his slacks and produces a folding knife. With his eyes still closed, he opens the knife and carefully slices off the eel's antennae, which float to the floor like dust. When he is done, the girl returns the eel to the tank. The creature comes to life and thrashes in the water, coiling and uncoiling, its body helpless to locate itself and its regular path, its fanged mouth open as if to scream. Water splashes from the tank and hits Peter's hand. The smell of brine is overpowering.

The girl takes the boy by the hand and leads him to a staircase on the opposite side of the room. They stop at the foot; the girl gestures to Peter. He walks between them and climbs the stairs.

He finds himself immediately in a room with no windows and no visible source for the soft light that fills it. There is a background wash of sound like air-conditioning but the room is the same temperature as the rest of the house. The room contains no furniture other than a large four-poster bed covered in loose white sheets on which Olivia lies supine. Her head and shoulders move gently as if to music; her hands flutter by her sides. Her legs are still. Her eyes are closed. Her lips form words but she does not speak. There is nothing random about her motions; they are orderly, purposeful.

Peter walks up to the bed and looks down at Olivia. She is smiling as her lips move. He considers lying down beside her but decides that would be a mistake. Instead he leaves her to whatever she has found, the music he cannot hear, and descends the stairs. He avoids looking at the tank; he cannot bear to see if the eel continues to thrash, or has resumed its ordered circuit, or floats motionless on top of the water. The children are not in the study or the living room or on the porch. He walks carefully down the outside steps and returns to the common.

The sun has set; the band is gone. Only their car remains. Peter sits back down on the same bench where he listened to the band's old music. He will make no effort to leave. He will wait for Olivia here in the mountains, in the darkness, in the silence beneath the cold and nameless stars.

ABOUT THE CONTRIBUTORS

STEVE RASNIC TEM is a past winner of the Bram Stoker, International Horror Guild, British Fantasy, and World Fantasy Awards. His most recent book is the collaboration *The Man on the Ceiling* with wife Melanie Tem, an expansion of their award-winning novella. In November Centipede Press will be publishing *In Concert*, a collection of all their collaborative short fiction.

STEVE ELLER lives in Seattle. On the occasional sunny day, he likes to sit on his rooftop deck and stare out over the bay. A bottle of Pyramid Hefeweizen might be found nearby. He shares his penthouse with a woman named Susan and two feline sisters, Sophie and Megan. He once won a Bram Stoker Award, but doesn't care to bring it up. He has season tickets for the Seahawks and Storm. He dedicates this story to Dr. Howard Leonard, PhD.

BECCA DE LA ROSA lives in Dublin, Ireland. Her fiction has appeared in *Strange Horizons, Lady Churchill's Rosebud Wristlet*, and *Fantasy Magazine*, among other places. Read more of her work online at www.beccadelaRosa.com.

STEPHEN GRAHAM JONES' most recent novel is *The Long Trial Of Nolan Dugatti.* It concerns a time traveling centipede, that in turn concerns us all. Before that it was the horror novel *Demon Theory.* Next up, *Ledfeather*, a love story with suicide. After that, a horror collection from Prime Books, *The Ones That Almost Got Away.* Then, the world. As for what Jones does besides read, and write about himself as if he's not in the room: he teaches fiction at CU Boulder.

KAREN HEULER's stories have appeared in anthologies and in dozens of literary and commercial magazines. She has published two novels and a short story collection, and has won an O. Henry award. Her latest novel, *Journey to Bom Goody*, concerns strange doings in the Amazon.

SETH LINDBERG has always disliked those one-paragraph biographies in the back of books, but the feeling might be mutual. He currently resides in California and has a fluffy cat named Sif.

VYLAR KAFTAN writes everything from hard sf to horror. Her work has appeared in *Realms of Fantasy, Clarkesworld*, and *Strange Horizons.* She lives in northern California. Visit her website at www.vylarkaftan.net.

STEVE BERMAN has been a finalist for both the Andre Norton Award for Young Adult Science Fiction and Fantasy (for his debut novel, *Vintage*) and a Lambda Literary Award (for the anthology *Charmed Lives*). He's sold over eighty articles, essays and short stories. He once stole a job from a *New York Times*-bestselling author (well, she wasn't all that at the time). He lives in southern New Jersey and does own a few hats.

LAVIE TIDHAR writes weird fiction. He grew up on a kibbutz in Israel and since lived in South Africa, the UK, and the remote Banks islands of Vanuatu, in the South Pacific. His short stories appeared in *Sci Fiction, Strange Horizons*, the World Fantasy Award winning anthology *Salon Fantastique* and many others.

NICK MAMATAS is the author of two novels, *Move Under Ground* and *Under My Roof*, both of which have been nominated for literary awards. His short fiction has appeared in *Mississippi Review, Weird Tales, ChiZine, Polyphony,* and in the slicks *Razor, Spex,* and *Nature.* Much of his recent work is collected in *You Might Sleep . . .* By the time you read this, Nick will be living in the California Bay Area.

MICHAEL CISCO is the author of *The Divinity Student* (winner of the International Horror Writers Guild award for best first novel of 1999), *The San Veneficio Canon, The Traitor*, and T*he Tyrant.* His short stories have appeared in *Leviathan, Album Zutique*, and the *Thackery T. Lambshead Pocket Guide to Eccentric and Discredited Diseases.* He lives in New York City.

GEOFFREY H. GOODWIN has had a story in *Rabid Transit* and *Not One of Us*, three in *Lady Churchill's Rosebud Wristlet* and two stories and three poems in *The Surgery of Modern Warfare*. Those are some of the cooler places that he remembers at the moment. Other good things have happened but everything is temporary and some braincells may have settled during shipment. He also interviews writers for the webzine *Bookslut*, has an MFA from The Jack Kerouac School of Disembodied Poetics at Naropa University in Boulder, Colorado and is a bookseller in Eastern Massachusetts. His iPod currently has more songs by Skinny Puppy than by any other artist and he can be reached at GeoffreyHGoodwin@aol.com or through his blog at http://readingthedark.livejournal.com.

CARRIE LABEN grew up on a small farm in Western New York. She now lives in Brooklyn with four cats and an amusing human. She actually really likes birds quite a lot, and blogs about them at pinguinus.wordpress.com. Her work has previously appeared in *Clarkesworld Magazine* and *Apex Digest Online*.

F. BRETT COX's fiction has appeared in *Century, Black Gate, North Carolina Literary Review, Lady Churchill's Rosebud Wristlet, Black Static, Postscripts*, and elsewhere. His essays and reviews have appeared in numerous publications, including *The New England Quarterly, The New York Review of Science Fiction, Science Fiction Studies, Science Fiction Weekly*, and *Paradoxa*. With Andy Duncan, he co-edited

Crossroads: Tales of the Southern Literary Fantastic (Tor, 2004). A native of North Carolina, Brett is Associate Professor of English at Norwich University in Northfield, Vermont. He lives in Roxbury, Vermont, with his wife, playwright Jeanne Beckwith.

ABOUT THE EDITORS

PAUL TREMBLAY, a two-time nominee of the Bram Stoker Award, has sold over fifty short stories to markets such as *Razor Magazine, Chizine, Weird Tales, Last Pentacle of the Sun: Writings in Support of the West Memphis Three*, and *Best American Fantasy 3*.

Along with his first novel *The Little Sleep*, he is the author of the short speculative fiction collection *Compositions for the Young and Old* and the hard-boiled/dark fantasy novella *City Pier: Above and Below*. He served as fiction editor of *Chizine* and as co-editor of *Fantasy Magazine*, and was also the co-editor (with Sean Wallace) of the *Fantasy, Bandersnatch*, and *Phantom* anthologies. *No Sleep till Wonderland*, the follow up to *The Little Sleep*, will be published in February, 2010. Paul has also served as a juror for the Shirley Jackson Awards and is currently an advisor. He lives outside of Boston, Massachusetts, has a master's degree in Mathematics, has no uvula, and he is represented by Stephen Barbara of Foundry Literary + Media.

SEAN WALLACE is the founder and editor for Prime Books, which won a World Fantasy Award in 2006. In his spare time he is also the co-editor of the Hugo- and World Fantasy Award-nominated *Clarkesworld Magazine* and critically-acclaimed *Fantasy Magazine*; the editor of the following anthologies: *Best New Fantasy, Fantasy, Horror: The Best of the Year, Jabberwocky*, and *Japanese Dreams*; and co-editor of *Bandersnatch, Phantom, Weird Tales: The 21st Century*, and *World of Fantasy: The Best of Fantasy Magazine*. He currently and happily resides in Rockville, MD, with his wife and two cats.